It was breathtaking. The snow-covered peaks sparkled in the setting sun, a clear sky above their heads.

Beneath them the lights of the village drew farther and farther away as the funicular rose. It felt as if they were flying.

"You like it?" Andrea was almost dancing on the spot.

"Yes, I love it." He put his arm around her shoulders. And then suddenly she turned and kissed him.

Cal drew back a little, gazing into her eyes. Gorgeous eyes that set the ever-changing beauty of the mountains to shame. He couldn't resist kissing her again, and this time she responded more urgently. As if this one moment was everything and she was going to wring every last drop of its potential from it.

It was everything. It had to be, because it couldn't be repeated. The thought only made Cal more determined, desperately seeking everything that he knew wouldn't happen again. He felt her shift in his arms, clinging to him tightly.

Dear Reader,

Most romances include a wedding—where would we be without the promise of that happy ending? But for this story I wondered how my hero and heroine would cope with having to help organize someone else's wedding.

Doctors Cal Lewis and Andrea Allinson have just one thing in common: they're both determined that their best friends' wedding will go off without a hitch. Everything's been carefully planned and prepared—what could possibly go wrong? But working together on the final preparations for the wedding is far more of a challenge than either of them could have imagined, and they find themselves stretched to their limits, both professionally and personally.

I loved finding out how two people trying to make the perfect day for their friends could find their own romance. Thank you for reading Cal and Andrea's story!

Annie x

THE BEST MAN
AND THE BRIDESMAID

ANNIE CLAYDON

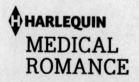

HARLEQUIN

MEDICAL
ROMANCE

HARLEQUIN®
MEDICAL
ROMANCE™

Recycling programs
for this product may
not exist in your area.

ISBN-13: 978-1-335-14978-7

The Best Man and the Bridesmaid

Copyright © 2020 by Annie Claydon

For questions and comments about the quality of this book,
please contact us at CustomerService@Harlequin.com.

Harlequin Enterprises ULC
22 Adelaide St. West, 40th Floor
Toronto, Ontario M5H 4E3, Canada
www.Harlequin.com

Printed in U.S.A.

Cursed with a poor sense of direction and a propensity to read, **Annie Claydon** spent much of her childhood lost in books. A degree in English literature followed by a career in computing didn't lead directly to her perfect job—writing romance for Harlequin—but she has no regrets in taking the scenic route. She lives in London: a city where getting lost can be a joy.

Books by Annie Claydon

Visit the Author Profile page
at Harlequin.com for more titles.

CHAPTER ONE

HE *WAS* HANDSOME. It was the first thing Andrea Allinson noticed about Cal Lewis, when he stepped into the hotel foyer. Maggie had gone into some detail when describing him, and the dark blond hair, tawny eyes and broad shoulders were all present and correct. Along with an indefinable quality that made Andrea catch her breath…

The hotel staff were homing in on their three newest guests like bees around a honeypot. The manager appeared from her office and shook everyone's hand, declaring that everything would be perfect for the wedding. Maggie looked dewy-eyed and excited, as any prospective bride should, and a little pink cheeked from the ride up here on the funicular railway. Her fiancé, Joe, caught her hand and raised it to his lips.

But Andrea couldn't take her eyes off Cal. He was standing a little to one side, allowing Maggie and Joe to be at the centre of everyone's attention. Smiling and… Handsome didn't really cover it. *Very* handsome, maybe, but that didn't account for the tingle that was running down Andrea's spine. *Love at first sight* might describe it, but Andrea was immune to that kind of thing. It was more likely just a severe case of physical attraction at first sight, which was awkward, but far more manageable.

Maggie caught sight of her, and broke away from the party, running towards Andrea and practically falling into her waiting arms.

'I'm so excited!'

Andrea hugged her friend tightly. This moment had been a long time coming, but now Maggie and Joe's wedding was just twelve days away. They'd met here, at the hotel in the Italian Alps where Andrea was the in-house doctor, and Joe and Maggie had decided that it was the perfect place for their wedding. In a little over a week's time family and friends would be arriving, but for the time being the wedding party consisted of just Maggie and Joe, along with Cal, who was Joe's best man.

'Everyone's been so kind.' Maggie's eyes were dancing with happiness. 'We had champagne on the plane, and then the man who operates that gorgeous train gave me this…'

Maggie displayed a red rose that was pinned to her coat, which had been a little squashed by the embrace. Andrea set it to rights, and then couldn't resist giving her friend another hug, which crushed the petals of the rose all over again.

'It's going to be perfect. I've got everything arranged at this end.' Andrea had been liaising with the hotel staff for months, determined that everything *would* be perfect for her friends.

'You're more worried about this than I am. It'll all be fine.' Maggie displayed an enviable optimism about the arrangements for her wedding, maybe because she'd been through so much to reach this point. 'As long as we're all here and we're happy and healthy, what can go wrong?'

Andrea had a list of all the things that could go wrong, but she wasn't about to share it with Maggie. Her friend had a point. As long as everyone was happy and healthy, what more could anyone want?

'And we'll have more than a week together before the big day to relax. I'm so looking forward to it…' Maggie hugged Andrea again, taking the opportunity to whisper in her ear. 'What do you think of him? He's rather lovely, isn't he?'

Maggie had already made it quite clear that

good looks were just the tip of the iceberg. Besides being handsome, Joe's best man was kind and had a good sense of humour. He had a fascinating job and was a doctor too, so he and Andrea would have lots in common and plenty to talk about. Maggie had been to his flat in London and considered it comfortable and stylish. And he was single…

That final detail made Maggie's intentions very clear. A flutter of romance between the head bridesmaid and the best man might be considered par for the course, but Maggie had obviously decided that Andrea needed a little shove in the right direction. As far as Andrea was concerned, Cal Lewis's best attribute might be his ability to turn a blind eye to Maggie's hints, because she wasn't interested.

'He's…you're right. Very handsome.' That was more than obvious, and saying anything different would be the kind of lie that attracted suspicion from her friend.

'And he's a really lovely guy.' Maggie's bright blue-eyed gaze searched Andrea's face. 'The kind someone might move on with?'

'Don't you worry about me. I have moving on in hand.' Andrea squeezed her friend's hand. It had been three years since Judd had died, and Maggie had been quite right when she'd gently suggested that maybe he would have wanted Andrea to move on with her life. But moving on was easy to wish for, and hard to do.

Maggie grinned at her. 'Well, in that case—'

She jumped as Andrea nudged her hard. Cal and Joe had been relieved of their cases, and were heading towards them. Which was a relief because it meant Andrea didn't have to listen to any more of the ways in which Cal was wonderful, and a new challenge because now she was going to have to look him straight in the eye.

'Andrea…' Joe greeted her with a hug. 'It was nice of you to get the welcoming committee out for us.'

'Everyone loves a wedding.' Andrea smiled up at Joe. He'd been a rock for Maggie over the last two years, and their shared concern for her had brought Andrea and Joe together and made them firm friends.

'And *this* is going to be the best wedding ever.' Maggie smiled up at her fiancé. 'Because *I'm* marrying *you.*'

Joe chuckled and kissed Maggie's cheek. 'We'll take the lovebirds thing elsewhere in a minute, before we bore everyone to tears with it. Andrea, meet Cal…'

Andrea ignored Maggie's excited smile. It was bad enough trying to dismiss the little thrill of excitement that coursed through her, and she was sure that any moment now she was going to blush...

'Andrea. It's a pleasure to finally meet you. Maggie's told me so much about you.'

He had a nice voice—soft and deep, like rich honey. Andrea took his outstretched hand, feeling the warmth of his fingers. As handshakes went, this one was pretty spectacular, as well.

She *was* blushing now. Maybe it would be better if she stopped trying to ignore the unwanted feelings that gripped her. Just take them for what they were—a momentary thrill—and hope that he would manage to do something unattractive enough to make them wither and die.

'Some of it good, I hope.' Andrea tried to make a joke, but it just sounded as if she was fishing for a compliment.

'I've been hoping all the way here that you might have just one or two faults that Maggie didn't mention. This is my first time as a best man, so I'm feeling my way with it.'

It was said with the kind of smile that turned it into a very nice compliment. Andrea swallowed down the lump in her throat.

'It's my first time as a bridesmaid too. I guess we'll just make our mistakes together, and hopefully no one will notice.'

This conversation was going in entirely the wrong direction. The thought of feeling her way with Cal and making a few mistakes was all-consuming.

But Maggie was looking extremely pleased at the way things were going. Smug, even. Andrea couldn't deny her this small pleasure.

'Why don't we all go for coffee? I'm sure you could do with one.'

Joe nodded, clearly about to agree, and Maggie grabbed his arm.

'We'd love to, wouldn't we, Joe?' Maggie gave an exaggerated look of dismay. 'But I was up really late last night packing, and we had an early start this morning. We've hardly slept, and I can't keep my eyes open. I just want to go and lie down for an hour.'

Joe smiled, clearly unable to deny Maggie anything. 'Yeah, now you mention it…' He took Maggie's hand, looking around for someone to show them to their room. 'Can we take a rain check?'

Cal nodded thoughtfully. Obviously he had something on his mind, and Andrea swallowed down the impulse to wonder exactly what he was thinking. Better to leave his thoughts out of the equation and concentrate on what she needed from him to make this wedding perfect.

'Would you mind if I took a rain check too? I have some emails that I really need to answer...'

'Cal! I thought you said that you were going to have a *holiday* with us!' Maggie shot him a reproachful look and then turned to Andrea with a confiding air. 'He's very important. Very busy...'

Cal winced. 'I'm not that important at all. My patients are, though; I'm sure Andrea understands that as well as I do.'

Would he just *stop*? Stop saying all the right things and do something that made him less... likeable. Wantable, if that was even a word. Andrea wasn't picky, anything that would harden her heart against him would do.

'Of course. I have a clinic later on this afternoon, and there are a few things I should do beforehand.' Not very important things, but no one needed to know that. 'I'll catch up with you all this evening...'

The steep, uphill path was caked with snow, which crunched under Cal's boots. He had woken early, and in the bright morning the mountains seemed to be a welcome reminder that the world kept turning, without any regard for his own small preoccupations.

He'd reckoned that he had everything under

control. That was the way he liked things. Two weeks off work, during which his bosses had suggested he consider their offer of a promotion. He'd get in a little skiing, help out with the wedding arrangements, and then have the pleasure of seeing his best friend marry the woman who made him supremely happy. If Maggie had teased him a little about how well he'd get along with the head bridesmaid, it was just a little harmless fun.

Then he'd seen Andrea. It was as if the busy hotel foyer had suddenly lost focus, and the only thing that was clear and bright was her. When the porter had tried to take his case, Cal had realised he'd been clenching his fingers so hard around the handle that his knuckles were white. He'd apologised and smiled at the man, then followed Joe over to where the women were standing.

He thought he'd seen the suspicion of a blush on her cheeks. Maybe the temperature *had* actually risen and the sudden warmth in his chest wasn't just the result of his racing heartbeat.

Cal had thought himself relatively fearless. But when faced with Andrea's blue-grey eyes, her soft, dark curls, and the feeling that somehow he'd known her all of his life, he'd run away...

Yesterday evening, he'd sent his apologies

to Joe and Maggie and ordered dinner in his room, writing a string of emails. This morning, he'd left the hotel early for a walk, telling himself that a little solitary exploration was what he always did when he found himself in a new place. These excuses were beginning to wear a little thin.

Climbing higher, he could see the hotel below him, the low sun glinting in the large windows that made the most of the stunning views. People were beginning to circulate on the veranda, and early morning skiers were heading for the slopes that surrounded the building. The funicular railway, that ran high over the rugged terrain between the hotel and the village at the foot of the mountain, seemed to glisten in the morning light.

Here, of all places, it felt as if he'd found something precious. Something he didn't understand. Cal had spoken with Andrea for a total of maybe five minutes, and yet every word, every glance, had embedded itself deep in his consciousness.

Cal shook his head and turned, lengthening his stride as he made his way up the steep path. It didn't matter if this was just a passing impression, or something real, his way forward was exactly the same. His inability to commit to a relationship had already hurt a very dear friend. He was bad news, and liking someone was no excuse for breaking the rule he'd made that relationships were best left alone.

He would, however, have to spend a fair bit of time with Andrea since they had a wedding to organise. And now that a little exercise had worked off the shock of feeling something—feeling so much—when he'd first seen her yesterday, he knew he should stop avoiding her. They would work together on the wedding, maybe share a quiet toast with each other when everything went off smoothly, and that would be that.

Piece of cake.

Cal's absence from dinner the previous evening had been half expected, but when Andrea joined Joe and Maggie for breakfast the next day and found them sitting alone, she couldn't help but feel a little disappointed.

'He's gone for a walk.' Maggie turned the corners of her mouth down. 'And then apparently he has to make some phone calls. I can't imagine what he finds to say that takes so long.'

Andrea glanced at Joe, for help. He understood...

'You know this job isn't a nine to five.' He

gave Maggie a smile. 'Would you want things any different?'

Maggie shrugged. 'No. Dedication's a very attractive trait. Within reason, I suppose...'

Andrea laughed. 'Dedication doesn't always listen to reason.'

She'd been dedicated once, to the work that she and Judd had shared. It had seemed a perfect match, living and working together, sharing the same ideals. It had started slowly, as a friendship, and then turned into love, gradually growing together, their work and their lives dovetailing neatly.

And then the accident had ripped everything away. She'd been unable to save Judd, and had lost, not only the one man who meant everything to her, but her own confidence in being able to make a difference. Coming here to take up a job that didn't stretch her professionally amongst people who were little more than acquaintances had helped her to heal and given her a measure of peace.

'You won't go back, will you? To Africa...' Maggie's face was suddenly serious.

'No, I don't think I will. Going to Africa was just...it was never really a choice; it was something I just knew would happen. I'll never regret it, or the things that I was able to do there. Or meeting Judd. But I'm not going back.'

'You did more than most of us, Andrea. This is your place now, and that's good too.'

Joe was a doctor, and he knew what her work here consisted of. He must also know that most of her days consisted of bumps and sprains, with the odd broken limb or case of flu to break the monotony. The sense of achievement in the face of heavy odds wasn't so great, but it was all that Andrea could do now, and it *had* to be enough.

'It is what it is. I like it here.'

'I still worry about you, stuck away up here in the mountains. Never meeting anyone...'

'Maggie...' Joe's voice contained a hint of warning. He clearly had his reservations about Maggie's new role as matchmaker.

'It's okay.' Andrea grinned at Joe. 'It's what friends are for.'

Maggie nodded in agreement. 'Of course it is. And Cal is...well, naturally Joe didn't choose him as his best man on that basis, but since he's here...'

Joe put his face in his hands, in an expression of fond exasperation. It was time to surrender gracefully, before Maggie managed to wring any definite promises from her.

'Okay. I heard you. And if I *do* manage to catch up with Cal before the wedding, I'll keep it in mind.' Andrea reached for the folder in her bag. 'And meantime, this is for you. All the arrangements for the wedding.'

'Ooh!' The folder had the desired effect of changing the subject and Maggie flipped through the pages. 'Thank you. This is *so* amazing. Look, Joe, there are stars...'

'The stars indicate who's supposed to be organising what. Pink are for you, Maggie, and blue is for Joe.'

Joe watched as Maggie turned the pages. 'They're all purple and green.'

'Look, here's your stag night. There's a blue one.' Maggie consulted the index and turned to the page.

'Oh, right.' Joe read the entry. 'So...apparently I just have to turn up?'

'That's right. The green stars are for Cal... or...whoever's up for organising it.' It seemed suddenly too presumptuous to ask anything of him.

'He did promise to do something. I think he'll appreciate the list of venues.' Joe smiled. 'Thank you so much, Andrea. This is fantastic.'

'I *told* you Andrea had everything under

control.' Maggie gave him a bright smile, flipping the pages. 'There you are, see. You have to turn up to the wedding, as well.'

Joe chuckled. 'Yeah. I'll be doing that, don't you worry…'

Cal. Green stars. The first had to be introduced to the second at some point. But it seemed that when Cal wasn't holed up in his room, writing emails, or going for early morning walks, he was on the phone. Presumably on calls that lasted a while, because he hadn't joined them for lunch, either.

There was only one conclusion, and it was inescapable. Since Joe had confirmed that his friend wasn't a hermit, and that he'd had several conversations with him since they'd arrived here, Cal must have caught wind of Maggie's matchmaking intentions and was avoiding her. Andrea couldn't help a sinking feeling in the pit of her stomach, accompanied by the sharp tang of disappointment. They were actually two very good reasons why she should keep her distance.

But the wedding wasn't going to organise itself and she was going to have to seek him out sooner or later. Andrea decided to leave that until after her afternoon surgery.

'Andrea.' For once, she hadn't been thinking

about him, and the deep, honey-soaked sound of his voice took her by surprise. The bunch of keys that she'd just taken from her handbag to lock the door of the medical suite dropped to the floor with a clatter.

'I'm sorry. I didn't mean to startle you.' Andrea had been about to bend for the keys, but he was there first. As he rose, she caught a hint of his scent. Soap-fresh and yet somehow carrying with it an image of hot nights. Her limbs entwined with his... Andrea swallowed hard as Cal dropped the keys into her hand.

'You didn't. Thank you.' It occurred to Andrea that he might be here for the medical suite, and not her. 'Is there something you needed? You're not sick, are you?'

'Actually, it's you I need.' He frowned suddenly, as if that was a little too blunt for his liking. 'I'm sorry I haven't been around much. I know I need to touch base with you over the arrangements for the wedding, and Joe tells me you have a folder.'

'Yes, I have.'

Good. Cal and the folder. Green stars. Forget about everything else.

'Maybe I could get you a coffee? Whenever you have a moment.'

'Now's good. I only had two people on my list for my surgery and so I have the rest of the afternoon free. I can go and fetch my folder, and join you in the main coffee lounge.'

He nodded. 'Thanks. That's good of you.'

As soon as she'd pointed him in the right direction for the coffee lounge, and watched him turn the corner out into the reception area, Andrea made for the back stairs, and the small apartment that was situated above the medical suite.

Even when he was relaxed and moving slowly, Cal had a kind of energy about him. It was evident in his face and the way he moved, and it held the tantalising promise that anything might be possible. Anything and everything.

Andrea made for the bathroom, splashing cold water onto her face. Anything and everything extended as far as Cal's duties as best man, and no further. There was no place for her wildly beating heart, nor for her fevered imagination; now more than ever she had to be cool and collected. If she showed Cal that she was just as immune to him as he was to her, they could find a way to work together and make sure this wedding went without a hitch.

'Okay.' She squinted at herself in the bathroom mirror, resisting the impulse to put a little lipstick on. 'You know what you have to do. Stop being such a teenager about it.'

* * *

The comfortable coffee lounge offered spectacular views of snow-capped mountains, reaching up towards a clear blue sky. Cal was sitting by the window, and Andrea hoped that the panorama would have its usual calming influence on her. Maybe even provide a topic of conversation, if there were any awkward silences.

He was just as mouth-wateringly handsome as he'd been ten minutes ago. Maybe more so—it was difficult to quantify it exactly, particularly when she was trying to ignore it.

'Joe tells me you already have everything well organised.' He rose, waiting for Andrea to sit down before he lowered himself back into his seat. 'I'm planning on following your instructions to the letter.'

Nice. He was obviously keen to lay down a few ground rules, and this one would make everything easier.

'Nothing's set in stone, and I don't want to tread on your toes, if there's anything that you were planning.' Andrea bit her tongue. Just a *thank-you* would have done; it wasn't necessary to invite any further discussion.

Cal nodded thoughtfully, turning with a smile to the waitress who brought their coffee. Foamy cappuccino, just the way she liked it. Andrea remembered that his parting shot had been to ask how she wanted her coffee, and he must have already ordered.

'How did you meet Maggie?' It seemed that Cal was just as keen as Andrea was to keep the conversation on the topic of their friends, which was a relief.

'We lived on the same road when we were children. We've been best friends since we were six. I hear you met Joe at medical school?'

'Yes, that's right. And you're the in-house doctor for this hotel complex...'

He stopped speaking, pressing his lips together as if he'd made a faux pas. Being the doctor here was just a fact, but the way they'd managed to veer into asking about each other so quickly was unsettling.

'Yes. I...um...' Andrea took a breath. 'I've brought the wedding folder.'

She reached into her bag, taking out Cal's copy of the folder and putting it down on the low table between them. He nodded, making no move to pick it up.

'It seems we've heard all about each other already.' He raised one eyebrow, as if he could say more, but was debating whether that was wise.

'Yes, I suppose so.' There wasn't much doubt that Maggie had told Cal as much about her as she'd told Andrea about him. She felt her ears begin to redden, and wondered what on earth Maggie had found to say.

He was studying her face, and she felt a flush begin to spread from the back of her neck. This was *very* awkward. Then suddenly he smiled and the ridiculous feeling that she'd known him all her life, and that it wouldn't do any harm to be honest with him, asserted itself. Andrea turned her attention to her coffee, picking up her cup. At the moment, distance seemed a lot less complicated than honest.

Then Cal spoke again.

'I'm getting the sense that Maggie hasn't confined her matchmaking efforts to just me.'

CHAPTER TWO

CAL HAD BEEN WONDERING how he might drop this into the conversation. Whether he even should. But he was going to have to spend time with Andrea, and she was clearly just as uneasy in his company as he was in hers.

Her reaction told him that he hadn't been wrong. She reddened suddenly, and almost spilled her coffee all over her sweater.

Watching her regain her composure was delightful. She flashed him a look that gave the impression that he'd taken her by surprise but it could all be laughed off. She put her coffee down again, staring at it. Then she turned her gaze straight onto him.

Beautiful blue-grey eyes. The kind that could reach down into a man's soul. It felt as if they *were* reaching into his soul.

'You've saved me the trouble of working out how to mention it to you.' She gave him a little smile and Cal felt his heart lurch, beating faster at her command. 'It's a little awkward, but Maggie doesn't really mean anything by it... Think of it as one of those wedding traditions that we don't have to comply with.'

She quirked her lips downwards suddenly, as if she'd said the wrong thing. Cal smiled, wondering if it would ever be possible for Andrea to say the wrong thing to him.

'That sounds good to me. We can practise non-compliance.' Andrea's charm meant that he'd have to practise a good deal before he got it perfect, but at least they were on the right track now.

'Because I've no intention of...um... I mean...' Andrea reddened furiously. 'I didn't mean that as an insult. It's me, not you.'

It was tempting to pretend he didn't know what she meant. Cal reminded himself that she must be suffering from an agony of embarrassment at the moment.

'I feel just the same. I'm far too set in my ways, and too busy to do any woman the rank disservice of asking her to be more than a friend. Least of all you.'

Somehow it all came out in vaguely understandable sentences, which was a surprise. All Cal was able to think about was the delicate pink of her cheeks, and how much he wanted to touch her skin.

But he'd managed to make his meaning clear. She puffed out a breath of relief.

'Nicely put. I feel the same. Only, I'm not terribly busy, it's more…' She gave a little shrug, the colour draining from her face suddenly. 'Bad break-up.'

Cal nodded. However much he wanted to ask, he should leave it at that. 'We understand each other, then.'

'Yes, we do.'

Why did he feel so disappointed? This was exactly what he'd wanted to happen. Cal brushed the question aside.

'I guess Maggie and Joe are so happy together that they have a hard time imagining anyone would choose anything else.' Cal ventured the observation, and Andrea nodded, smiling.

'That's right. They met when Maggie came here on holiday to visit me. She said she knew he was the one and kept apologising for spending so much time with him and not me. But I was really happy for her.'

'I remember Joe saying something of the sort when he got home. He told me he'd met the woman he wanted to marry. And then two weeks later Maggie told him she didn't want anything more to do with him.'

'She had her reasons. Joe told you…?' Andrea shot him a querying look and Cal nodded. 'She'd just found out that she had breast cancer and she didn't want Joe to feel he had to stick with her.'

'He had no choice. Being there for Maggie wasn't something he even had to think about, he knew that was what he wanted. I told him if that was the way he felt, he needed to stop moping around and convince Maggie of that.'

Andrea chuckled, leaning back in her seat, suddenly at ease. 'And I told her that if she really wanted to be with him, she might consider giving him the benefit of the doubt, and believing him when he said he wanted to be there for her. So I guess we should both take a little of the blame for this wedding.'

That explained a lot. Why Joe had been so sure that Maggie wouldn't change her mind, and then suddenly she had. Cal felt the muscles at the side of his jaw begin to relax. It seemed that he and Andrea felt the same way about more than one thing.

'I'm very happy to do that.'

'Me too.'

'In that case…' He leaned forward, picking up the wedding folder. 'I think I have some reading to do, to catch up.'

'Perhaps I should leave you to it. We can meet up again later.' It seemed that Andrea wanted out of here suddenly and she sprang to her feet. Having her close prompted much the same set of conflicting feelings in Cal's heart. He couldn't bear the thought of her leaving, but he knew that it would bring relief from having to constantly remind himself that he mustn't reach forward and touch her hand.

Whatever she wanted to do was fine with him. He should let her know that he'd be there when she wanted him, and not when she didn't. Cal supressed a smile at the irony of the notion. Allowing someone else to dictate his actions was new territory for him.

'Shall we discuss it a bit more over dinner?'

Andrea hesitated, and when she nodded, gratification swelled through Cal's heart. 'Yes, dinner would be okay. The hotel has a crepe bar and a pizzeria. The restaurant's nice too.'

'How about the restaurant?' He had no doubt that pizzas or crepes would be good options, but a restaurant implied three courses and a little more time to sit and talk. To drink in Andrea's way of getting straight to his heart.

'Yes, that's fine.' She didn't hesitate. It seemed that Andrea had no objections to spending a little more time with him. 'Eight o'clock?'

'That sounds good. I'll see you then.'

He watched her go. Not as a courtesy, in

case she turned, but because he couldn't drag his gaze away from her, or from the entrance to the coffee lounge, until he was absolutely sure that she wasn't going to return.

Cal Lewis. Out of control and craving one last glimpse of a woman. If Cal had confided that to Joe he would have seen the irony of it too. Maybe made a smiling enquiry about whether this was love at first sight, which Cal would have rejected out of hand.

Because Cal had always been *in* control. His parents' tug of love with each other had turned into a tug of war when Cal was ten and they'd divorced. From then on it had been a matter of having to steer a centre course between two parents who had each wanted him to take their side.

Cal had learned to ignore their differing ambitions for him, and quietly pursue his own course. If love meant he had to live his life according to someone else's aspirations, then he wanted no part of it. He'd dedicated himself to his studies, and then to his work, never allowing a woman to entwine him in the sticky threads of commitment.

And then, Mary. She'd been a good friend, and Cal had thought they saw eye to eye. She knew his track record, and it was she who'd suggested their on-off relationship as being the obvious answer for two busy people. Then she'd fallen in love, and Cal hadn't.

He had no excuses for hurting Mary so badly. He'd cared for her deeply, but he hadn't loved her, and he didn't know how to give what she was asking of him.

'There's something missing in you, Cal...'

He felt Mary's words had been slightly unfair because the thing that was missing in Cal was the very thing that had attracted her to him in the first place. But the words could be forgiven, because they had come from a place of hurt, and they were true. Love took compromise, bending to fit with another person's life and values, and he just didn't have that in him. He would never hurt someone again the way he'd hurt Mary.

He flipped open Andrea's folder. Love was for other people, not for him. He might be a control freak when it came to guiding his own destiny, unwilling to compromise and unable to commit, but at least he knew what he was. And for the next two weeks, he was Joe's friend, here to help with the wedding.

Really? Andrea hadn't spent more than half an hour with Cal, and already it seemed she'd entered into some kind of collusion with him. She'd come dangerously close to mentioning the hurt that she never talked about, and which she'd come here to escape. And then…

Then he'd said they understood each other. And Andrea's agreement hadn't been born from a wish to be polite—she felt that Cal really did understand her, and that she understood him. Which was ridiculous, because she hardly knew him.

It's done now. Get on with it.

Andrea murmured the words to herself as she walked towards the large suite that Maggie and Joe were occupying. She didn't have to examine every little thing that they'd both said so closely. She should concentrate on the matter in hand.

She found Maggie alone in the suite, the crumpled bedcovers and the book which lay open on the pillows showing that Maggie was doing exactly what Andrea wanted her to: relaxing. But now it seemed that Maggie not only wanted to talk, she wanted every detail of Andrea's meeting with Cal.

'You're having *dinner* with him, then.' Maggie made it sound as if sitting at the same table while eating was exciting and seductive. Andrea had been trying to convince herself it was neither exciting nor seductive ever since the idea had been mooted.

'Someone's got to keep him company. And

I'm starting to feel that three's a crowd where you and Joe are concerned.'

'Never.' Maggie reached forward, pulling Andrea down to sprawl on the bed with her. 'Three's just right when it's you.'

'It's nice of you to say so. But you and Joe are on your own for this evening.'

'Hmm.' Maggie was clearly pleased by the thought. 'Where are you going?'

'What, so you can book a table and keep me under surveillance?'

'No!' The thought had obviously occurred to Maggie. 'So we can go somewhere else and leave you in peace.'

'You don't need to do that either. But we will be talking about the wedding, so you and Joe aren't invited. We're going to the main restaurant.'

'Very nice. Okay, so I think I fancy something light this evening. Crepes, maybe.'

'Or you could have room service. Oysters and champagne…?' Andrea teased her friend.

'That's a thought. Although Joe isn't a big fan of oysters, we might just have the champagne…' Maggie quirked the corners of her lips down. 'I'm being a pain, aren't I?'

'Yes.' Andrea leaned forward, hugging her friend. 'But don't ever give up on me, will you? I'd hate that.'

'I just want you to be happy. Cal's a lovely guy, but it's not really about him. You'll never know what you want if you don't get out and meet new people.'

Andrea swallowed down the temptation to say that it was *all* about Cal at the moment. All about that nagging feeling that maybe she was a little stuck, and that Cal had the power to pull her free. She already knew what she wanted, and it was her quiet little life here. Calm and uneventful, it had given her the ability to function when the world she'd known, the world she'd chosen, had been torn apart.

'It's all about possibilities.'

Maggie was all smiles now. 'Yeah. Possibilities…'

They'd already unpacked Maggie's wedding dress, and hung it carefully in the wardrobe, but a small second case still lay untouched on the luggage rack. Andrea got to her feet, and lifted it over onto the bed.

'You're going to Bridesmaidzilla me again, aren't you?' Maggie's grin told Andrea that she didn't mind in the slightest.

'Someone has to. I want to make sure you've brought everything, so I can tick a few things off my list.'

'You don't need to go and try on some options for what to wear for dinner?' Maggie shot her an innocent look.

'No. It doesn't take me three hours to decide what to wear for anything; my wardrobe isn't that big.' Something to take her mind off dinner, until Andrea absolutely *had* to think about it, was a much better modus operandi.

'Whatever you say.' Maggie sat up, unzipping the suitcase.

Cal had thought about wearing a suit, but decided that would be far too formal. When he arrived in the hotel's large restaurant, it was obvious that his choice of an open-necked shirt and sweater blended in with everyone else here, and waiting for Andrea to arrive gave him the opportunity to wonder why on earth he'd given the matter a second thought. What to wear didn't usually come so high on his list of priorities.

He saw her enter, stopping to speak to one of the waiters, who pointed her in the right direction. Cal couldn't help watching as she hurried towards him.

The dark curls around her face, her blue-grey eyes, were a stunning and ever-changing form of beauty. Her dark blue top and trousers couldn't hide the way she moved, and seemed to be an exercise in understated perfection.

She would have been perfect anywhere, wearing anything.

He rose as she approached and she smiled awkwardly, before regaining her composure. A waiter pulled back her seat for her, and she turned to make eye contact with him as she thanked him. Cal almost begrudged the man those few moments of her attention.

'Sorry I'm late. I've been helping Maggie unpack the rest of the things she brought for the wedding.'

'Everything's survived the journey?' Joe had almost knocked someone over in his eagerness to get to the luggage carousel at the airport, and reclaim the cases that held Maggie's wedding dress, and other unspecified items that were necessary for the wedding.

'Yes. We unpacked the wedding dress yesterday and it has a couple of little creases but they'll steam out. Everything else is all present and correct, so I can tick all of that off my list.'

Cal had spent the last few hours acquainting himself with Andrea's lists, and the folder she'd given him lay ready on the table. The first page covered the arrangements for yesterday, and quite a few details that had seemed to him to have happened by chance turned out to have been carefully planned: the hotel minibus that had turned up just at the right moment;

the ride on the funicular railway that had been waiting for them at the station; even the rose that the conductor had presented Maggie with was there, and had been neatly ticked off.

Then there were pages to track the arrival of guests and family, which rooms were booked for them, along with dietary requirements and special arrangements for children and the elderly members of the wedding party. The cake had been made and was apparently stored in the hotel's kitchen. The venues for the wedding and reception, both of which were to be held here at the hotel, had been photographed and there was a seating plan, along with an itinerary for the wedding day.

'Your folder's impressive. You've done something like this before?' The whole thing smacked of maximum forethought and minimum fuss.

'No. But it's much the same as arranging anything, isn't it?'

'I suppose so.' The clinic that Cal worked for could do with the kind of attention to detail and organisational ability that was displayed here. If Andrea was as good a doctor as she was a wedding organiser, then her talents were wasted on sprains and bruises at a smart skiing resort.

'If there's anything I've missed...' The way

her lower lip quivered slightly at the thought of something that had escaped her attention was delightful.

'I can't think of a thing. I'll follow up on your list of places to go for the stag night.'

She blushed a perfect shade of embarrassed pink. 'I…um… I didn't want to step on your toes, but I thought… Just in case you didn't already have somewhere in mind…'

'No, I had nowhere in mind. I was going to ask you for some suggestions, along with the number of a local cab company.' The relevant page had the numbers of three taxi services, typed in a clear, bold font, presumably in an attempt to counteract any blurred vision that might occur at the end of the evening.

'Ah. Well, it's all there, and you've got plenty of time to scout them out.'

Cal wondered if Andrea might be persuaded to go with him. As he turned the thought over in his mind, it seemed far too precious to dismiss entirely, and he decided to put it on hold in favour of ticking another few items off Andrea's list.

'I have the rings, they're locked in the safe in my room. And I saw your email about photographs. I have some old ones of Joe from our time at medical school.'

She gave him a thrilling smile. 'Perfect.

I have loads of Maggie from when we were growing up, and it'll be nice to include a few embarrassing ones of Joe as well.'

'I'll let you sort through them.' Cal picked up the menu, raising one eyebrow. 'Any suggestions?'

She laughed, just as she was meant to. 'No, I'm not that much of an organisational freak. You're on your own with that.'

Ordering their meal, eating it, and discussing the arrangements set out in her folder carried them through the next hour, but coffee brought one of those awkward silences.

'So...' Andrea cleared her throat awkwardly. 'What do you do? Apart from being a doctor, I mean...'

She wanted to go there? Cal had kept the conversation deliberately impersonal in an attempt to make it clear that he wasn't about to embarrass her by going along with Maggie's plans for them. But her interest prompted a pleasant tingling feeling at the back of his neck.

'I work for an organisation based in London, which specialises in helping patients worldwide who don't have access to the medical facilities they need.'

'Really?' Something ignited behind the cool blue-grey of Andrea's eyes. 'Tell me more...'

Maybe he shouldn't. Cal's work was the one area in his life he was passionate about, and he'd promised that passion should have no part in his relationship with Andrea. But he couldn't help himself.

'We have a two-pronged strategy. We have facilities for complex surgeries in London, and part of my work is to assess referrals from doctors overseas and care for patients there.'

Andrea nodded. 'And the other part?'

'Simple, everyday surgeries, available locally, can make an enormous difference. We work to provide surgical support to doctors and patients in their own countries. That's done partly by travelling surgical teams, but mainly by helping build facilities and providing the equipment that's needed. Along with maintenance, of course.'

Andrea smiled, suddenly. 'That's the crucial part, isn't it? Often it's the supply of spare parts for things like X-ray machines which is the most problematic.'

So she understood the issues. And she cared about them—Cal could see that in her face.

'Yes. We pledge to maintain the equipment we supply and a lot of our effort goes into that.'

'And what's your role exactly? Are you based in London?'

The desire to tell her everything about himself was as strong as the yearning to touch her. Stronger maybe, because it felt so much more personal.

'I spend about half my time in London, and half at our projects worldwide. My role's a mixture of surgical work and patient care, along with planning and strategy.'

He could almost feel her gaze tingling across his cheek, before it dropped to his hands, and then retreated to her own fingers, resting twined together on the table between them.

'It sounds like a very rewarding job.'

'It is. It's difficult sometimes, not being in one place for any appreciable length of time...' He fell silent. The stock excuse for his solitary lifestyle felt awkward at the moment. As if it broke the connection that had formed between them.

'Yes. I imagine so. You chose your job over your personal life, then?' Andrea was looking at him now, as if the answer meant something to her.

'I guess so. Not consciously, but that's the way things have worked out.'

She raised one eyebrow. Maybe she saw straight through him, and knew that he'd thought about it more than he would admit. That he'd always struggled with relationships, and then when he'd hurt Mary so badly, he'd decided to back away from that side of his life.

'Consciously enough that you know you're not going there, though.'

Maybe she was looking for reassurance, that what he'd said about not wanting a relationship wasn't just a reaction to Maggie's matchmaking, but a decision that he stuck to.

'Yeah. Enough for that. What about you?' Quid pro quo.

'Me?' She gave a little shrug. 'I thought the world was full of choices when I left medical school. I had a great job and I was engaged to someone I worked with. Then it all went rather badly wrong and… This is my happy place.'

Which rather supposed that everywhere else was Andrea's unhappy place. Cal wondered just how badly something had to go wrong for that to happen. The impression she gave, that everything was under control, seemed to be just a protective shell. Beneath it she was vulnerable, and that was one very good reason for Cal to keep his distance.

'It's…a beautiful place to be happy in.' Outside, the floodlights illuminated a winter's fairy-tale landscape, and during the day the view from here would be as spectacular as all the other views from the hotel's windows.

'Not always as fulfilling as I'd like. But yes,

it's a beautiful place.' There was a sadness in Andrea's tone that seemed to betray a knowledge that she could do more. At least he still had a world full of good places, and it seemed a shame that someone like her should have settled for so little.

A little shake of her head indicated that she was done with that conversation, though. However much he wanted to pursue it, it was important that Cal respected her boundaries.

'Have you tried snowboarding?' She was staring out of the window.

'No. I'm hoping to get a little skiing in, though.'

'I've never tried it either.' She gave a little shrug. 'Which is actually quite outrageous, given that I've been living here for two years now. Maggie and Joe have a lesson booked tomorrow morning and I was thinking of going with them…'

The unasked question hung in the air between them. It suddenly felt that Cal had been missing out on something all his life, and that snowboarding was the one and only thing he needed to do tomorrow.

'Do you know if there's a spare place in the class?'

'I did happen to check.' She twisted her mouth in a flash of dry humour. 'Yes. There is.'

This was okay. He didn't need to avoid Andrea, as if she were some dangerous creature that could rock his whole world. Cal could get to know her a little, and still stay within the boundaries he'd set for himself, because she had boundaries too. He'd stuck to his life plan up till now, and he could keep doing so.

'It would be remiss of me to pass that opportunity up, then. What time tomorrow...?'

CHAPTER THREE

THIS WAS *NOT* a date. Andrea had that thought firmly fixed in her mind. Maggie and Joe would be there, and if three was a crowd, then four was a positive army of people. She and Cal were on the same page with this, neither of them were minded to take any notice of Maggie's matchmaking. It was going to be just fine.

Even so, the look in Maggie's eyes when Cal had mentioned over breakfast that he'd be joining them this morning had said it all. Learning a new skill that would likely end up with her falling flat on her face was perhaps best avoided if romance was on the cards. Even Joe had looked quietly appalled.

But then, this wasn't a date. When the class had been divided into two, it was okay that Maggie and Joe were in the other group. And Cal betrayed none of that eagerness to impress that might spark the tinderbox of Andrea's fears.

'Slowly…' She heard Francine, the instructor, murmur quietly as he tackled the downhill slope for the first time. He was almost at the bottom when he fell, prompting a shock of concern that made Andrea clap her hand over her mouth. But then he climbed to his feet, grinning, and brushing the snow from his jacket.

'Don't do it like that. Watch out for your shoulder,' Francine reminded Andrea as she positioned herself at the top of the slope.

Andrea nodded. The temptation to forget all about the old injury to her left shoulder, and the craving for the same kind of fearlessness that Cal showed, should be resisted. She wasn't unbreakable any more.

But her shoulder was stable now, and she'd remembered to wear a support under her jacket, just in case. If the worst came to the worst, then at least there was a doctor on hand…

The thought of Cal having to snap her shoulder back into its proper position was far worse than any pain she might experience. That wasn't going to happen. She wasn't going to fall.

Her first attempt at the beginners' course was a little slower than everyone else's, but she managed to keep her balance. Cal was waiting at the bottom, and gave her a delicious smile.

'Nice one.'

Andrea quirked her lips down. She'd made it to the bottom, but not without compromise. 'I didn't go as fast as you…'

'Francine told us to go slowly for starters. I should have listened.'

'Is that an option for you? Giving it less than one hundred per cent?' The words slipped out. For some reason it was proving easy to treat Cal as if she'd known him all her life, and Andrea had to keep reminding herself that he was really just an acquaintance.

He chuckled as if they *had* known each other all their lives. They walked back up the slope together in companionable silence, but he'd clearly taken the comment to heart. When it was Cal's turn to try again, he shot her a conspiratorial smile, holding up seven fingers.

Giving it seventy per cent worked. He made it to the bottom without falling and Francine gave a nod of approval.

Maybe it was the thumbs-up sign he'd aimed in her direction from the bottom of the slope that had made her knees wobble with pleasure. Maybe it was because she sensed he was watching her every move as she prepared for her second descent. Or maybe she just hit a bump in the snow…

The feeling of falling dragged a panicked

cry from her lips. She hit the ground, rolling over onto her shoulder, and a growling pain reminded her that she'd been tempted past the limits that she'd set for herself.

'I'm okay. I'm okay…' She felt a hand on her arm, and knew it was Cal's.

'Sure you are. Stay down for a moment and catch your breath.' His voice was very close, and very reassuring. Andrea opened her eyes, focussing on his face.

That gaze. The one that seemed to know her through and through, and which seemed to accept everything it saw. It was probably just an illusion, but it felt all too real. She took a breath, and as the shock of falling subsided, her shoulder began to throb.

'Anything starting to hurt now?' He was on one knee, next to her.

'Um… No, I think I'm all right.' Andrea's hand drifted to her shoulder before she could stop it and she saw that Cal hadn't missed the gesture.

'Your shoulder?'

'It's fine,' she replied quickly and he raised his eyebrows.

'Is that one hundred per cent fine?'

Andrea ignored him, sitting up in the snow. 'Give me an arm up, will you?'

He leaned forward, his arm coiling around

her waist. That wasn't quite what Andrea had meant, but the feel of his body against hers was enough to silence any protest. And she had to admit that it was the most efficient way of propelling her to her feet.

'Okay?' Cal was very close, his arm still protectively around her.

'Yes. Thanks. Okay.' His scent rendered anything approaching a sentence out of the question. When he let her go, she couldn't step away from him for a moment. Cal's bulk, the sheer strength of his body, was mesmerising.

Then he stepped back. Andrea watched as he retrieved her snowboard, tucking it under his arm along with her own. One more small intimacy that only seemed to fuel the one massive intimacy that was growing in her imagination.

They walked together back up to the top of the slope. From here, they could see the steeper slopes, planted with yellow-and-black warning flags after last night's snowfall. And despite them, two figures were weaving their way down, their paths criss-crossing in the pristine layer of snow.

'Francine…' Andrea turned and Francine looked up, her face hardening as she saw the snowboarders.

'*Arrêtez…!* I told them to stay off that slope

this morning, but some people just can't resist fresh powder.' Francine turned to the other instructor. 'Bruno, will you finish up here for me?'

But it was already too late. As Francine made for one of the skidoos that was parked at the top of the ridge, one of the snowboarders seemed to waver from the precise formation, crashing into the other. As they both fell, a layer of snow seemed to detach itself, sliding after them.

She heard Francine's curse as she ran for the skidoo. The snowboarders were tumbling down the slope, but couldn't stay ahead of the rumbling mass of snow that followed them.

Bruno had already reached the skidoos, and started one of them up. Francine jumped on the back, hanging onto him as he set off around the curve of the ridge. Andrea made for the second skidoo, knowing without having to look that Cal was hard on her heels.

'Did you see where they fell?'

'Right there.' Cal pointed to a spot at the bottom of the slope. He was waiting for her to take her lead, and his confidence in her chipped away at her own fears.

'Okay, keep your eye on that spot while I drive. It's easy to get disoriented, and we have to find them fast…'

No more explanation was needed. Cal nodded, grabbing one of the helmets that hung from the handlebars, and Andrea climbed onto the skidoo. She put her own helmet on, and twisted the ignition key, feeling the all too welcome warmth of his body as he climbed onto the narrow seat behind her.

She followed in the tracks of Bruno and Francine's skidoo, knowing that they'd be taking the safest and most direct route to the fallen snowboarders. As they neared the bottom of the steep incline, Andrea could see a bright red flash of clothing as a figure got unsteadily to its feet. It looked as if one of the snowboarders had escaped relatively unharmed, but she couldn't see the other.

'Help us… Help…' It was a man's voice, filled with panic and desperation. Francine stopped the skidoo next to him, and he almost collapsed into her arms. Bruno sat him down, talking to him.

'He says he's okay.' Francine jogged across to Andrea as she got off the skidoo. 'Bruno will make sure, while we look for the other one.'

'Okay. Cal…' Andrea turned to find him but he wasn't there. Cal was trekking away from them, in a determined line across the snow.

'Here.' He stopped suddenly, turning towards them. 'I last saw them here.'

Francine gave him a nod of approval. 'Good. Then we start looking a little lower down.'

'Have we called for reinforcements?' Cal returned to where Andrea was standing, and murmured the words to her.

'Yes, Francine's got an alarm pager that she uses if anything happens on the slopes. They'll be here soon. We have drills every month, so everyone knows what to do. Do you have your transceiver with you? You'll need to switch it off now.'

He nodded, pulling the small unit out from under his sweater, and fiddling with it to switch it off, so that its signal wouldn't override that of the person who was buried in the snow.

'Great idea to have the hotel give these out to anyone going out on the slopes.' He grinned at Andrea. 'Yours?'

His smile was good to have, especially now that her suggestion that the hotel made sure everyone was carrying transceivers might save someone's life. 'It's part of our new safety plan.'

'Can I assume that was your idea too? Since you seem to know what everyone's about to do next.'

She felt a blush starting to reach up from the back of her neck, towards the cool air on her cheeks. Cal had seen past the swift reactions to the carefully constructed plan that Andrea had put into place.

'It's part of my job. Prevention is always better than a cure.'

He nodded. Andrea had done everything she could to avoid facing another life-or-death situation alone, and there was something very reassuring about Cal's presence—the way he was so calm, and yet ready to throw off that relaxed way of his at a moment's notice.

Francine was skiing in a wide circle, trying to locate the transceiver signal from the person buried in the snow. It must be ten minutes now...

The vision of Judd, so badly injured that she'd been unable to do anything for him, brought tears to her eyes. Then panic began to seep steadily into her body, fuelled by the low throb of pain in her shoulder. She was losing it, letting her fears govern her actions.

'Do the skidoos carry something we can dig with?' Cal's voice cut through the visions in her head.

'Um... Yes.' Andrea hung onto the calm in his voice, feeling it pull her back into the here and now. 'I'll get the kits.'

Shaking, she unpacked the probes and shovels from the skidoo, handing Cal one of each. 'You know how to use the probe?'

'Right angles to the surface, and feel for soft resistance?' Clearly he did, but he was checking with her. Or maybe he'd seen her falter, and was checking *on* her.

'Yes, that's right. As soon as Francine gets a hit on the transceiver, we can spread out and probe...'

Francine's voice sounded, and Andrea turned to see her signalling from a spot ten metres further down from where Cal had indicated. He'd done well in remembering it so precisely; it had shaved precious minutes off the time needed to find the buried snowboarder. Bruno was running over to join them now, and the small rescue party spread out and began to carefully probe the snow.

'Got something.' Cal fell to his knees, starting to dig with his hands. Almost immediately, he uncovered what looked like a discarded glove, but when he took hold of it the fingers gripped his tight. Cal started to clear the snow with his other hand, and Andrea ran to help him.

He wasn't letting go. Good. His tight grip was the one thing that gave the person beneath the snow hope at this moment. Andrea dug frantically, ignoring the sudden pain in her shoulder, and Francine and Bruno ran to help her.

She uncovered the second arm, this one thrown up as if to protect someone's face. When she moved it, she saw a woman's features, dazed and frightened. She was struggling to breathe, and Andrea tried to move the snow that covered her chest, while Cal cleared the snow from her face.

Pain shot through her shoulder again, so bad this time that it momentarily paralysed her arm. Andrea groaned and saw Cal's gaze flip up towards her.

'Shield her face, while Francine and Bruno dig.' No questions asked. Just a quick assessment of the situation, and exactly what was needed.

Andrea shifted along, carefully protecting the woman's face as Cal and the others dug furiously. The woman's chest was quickly exposed, and slow, shallow breaths turned into a deep gasp for air. Then she began to cry.

'Okay… You're okay.' Andrea tried to comfort her, in English first and then French. When she tried Italian, the woman's eyes opened suddenly, frightened and imploring.

'She's breathing better now.' The woman's lips were blue from the cold and lack of oxygen, but now that the pressure of snow on her chest was removed she could draw breath.

Cal nodded. 'It looks as if she landed feet first. We'll have to dig down a little further to free her legs.'

They'd cleared just the first hurdle. The woman was alive and breathing, but there was no way of knowing what injuries she'd sustained. They had to get her out before the effects of shock and cold weakened her even further.

Cal and Bruno were shovelling snow, while Francine moved the quickly growing piles back and out of their way. Bruno was trained for this, but Cal kept pace with him, tirelessly. Andrea kept a tight hold on the woman's hand, shielding her face and speaking to her to reassure her.

She could hear the deep growl of the snow ambulance, distant at first and now closer. The fully tracked vehicle carried the rescue and medical equipment needed to get the woman off the slope and transport her back down to the hotel, and it had brought reinforcements too. Two men grabbed the shovels from Cal and Bruno and they both moved back, breathless from their exertions.

'That's enough.' Cal's voice sounded, and Andrea looked around as silence fell. The woman's legs had been uncovered, and everyone stood back as he reached down into the deep well in the snow.

His examination was quick, but as thorough as the conditions allowed. He could only check for the most obvious of injuries at this stage, and Andrea watched the woman's face carefully for any signs of pain.

'Can we move her?' Cal's gaze connected with hers suddenly. With his expertise to help her, Andrea felt equal to the decision.

'Yes.' She looked up at the paramedic who had arrived with the snowcat. 'Tomas, we'll take spinal injury precautions.'

Tomas nodded. He already had everything ready, and passed a neck brace to Cal. Andrea reassured the woman, stepping back to allow Cal and Tomas room to work.

They'd done it. Together. She'd been so close to giving into the blurred panic that robbed her of her ability to help others, but Cal had been there for her, and Andrea had managed to keep functioning. The collective sigh of relief as the woman was lifted from the hole seemed to be a milestone for her, as well as their patient.

Andrea hesitated before climbing aboard the snowcat, reaching out awkwardly to grab the handhold with her right hand. Without thinking, Cal reached for her, boosting her up into the vehicle. Concern for the woman buried in the snow had driven everything else from his mind, but now that she'd been strapped into the carrycot and transported to the snow ambulance, he had a moment to think about Andrea.

The smooth, effective procedures were Andrea's doing. She was no stranger to taking on emergency situations, and when she'd faltered it hadn't been through any lack of experience. Too much experience, maybe. He'd seen the look in her eyes, the long-distance stare that focussed back onto something else, beyond the situation that had presented itself today.

'It all went rather badly wrong.'

He'd seen the evidence of her words, today. Not in her actions, but in her face. Suddenly Cal wanted to know *what* had gone so wrong for her.

But those questions could wait. There were more pressing issues on his mind now. Tomas had taken charge of the other snowboarder, helping him into the snow ambulance and strapping him into a seat.

'How's your shoulder?' he asked.

Andrea was now bending over the young woman they'd lifted from the snow, reassuring her. If Cal had seen that this was hard for her, she'd given no suggestion of that to their patient.

'It's okay. An old injury…'

'You sit.' He indicated the spare seat, next to Tomas. 'I'll keep an eye on our patient on the way down.'

She nodded. Andrea knew her limitations, and that Cal would find it easier to grab hold of something to steady himself as the snow ambulance transported them down to the clinic. The feeling of being part of a jigsaw puzzle, and fitting neatly together with the people he worked with, wasn't new to Cal. But when it had happened with Andrea, there was a level of intimacy that he hadn't experienced before.

The woman was drowsy still, alternating between moments of extreme distress and listlessness. Cal was rather more worried about the listlessness, as distress was a natural reaction to the terrifying experience of being buried alive. The snow ambulance was well equipped, and he busied himself with basic checks on her status, trying to reassure her as he did so.

'Va tutto bene.' He heard Andrea's voice behind him, giving him the Italian words that he was struggling to recollect. He repeated them, and saw the woman calm a little.

The vehicle came to a halt and Andrea was

first off, climbing down awkwardly. He and
Tomas lifted the carrycot carefully and he
found himself in a covered area with swing
doors at the far end. Andrea held them open,
and he helped carry the woman through into
a large and well-equipped medical bay.

Andrea spoke to a woman who came to
meet them, then turned to Tomas to ask him
to take charge of the other snowboarder. The
she turned to Cal.

'The air ambulance will be here in fifteen
minutes. Which means we have some time to
prepare her for the ride.'

'Okay. Gentle warming and observation?'

Andrea nodded. 'Yes, I think so.'

She took charge of the paperwork, writing
everything down in a neat, precise hand. The
woman's name was Giulia, and now that they
were here Cal could see that she was little more
than a girl. She had no relatives here at the
hotel and had come with a group of friends,
who had all gone out to the local village this
morning. The hotel staff had called them, but
they wouldn't be back until the funicular railway delivered its next group of passengers.

As warmth began to penetrate her body,
Giulia began to cry and Andrea comforted her
tenderly. Cal kept a close eye on the screen that
displayed her vitals, and when he removed her

boots her ankle was a dark purplish colour and began to swell almost immediately. Andrea pointed him towards a cupboard, which he found held every kind of splint imaginable, and he chose a temporary inflatable cast for Giulia's ankle.

She'd be in good hands. When the air-ambulance crew arrived, they were kind and efficient, and Andrea clearly knew them, so he was happy to leave Giulia in their care. As the helicopter rose from its landing pad on the roof, Andrea turned to him, scooping her curls back from her face.

'Thanks for your help.' She twisted her mouth down. 'So much for you being on holiday.'

'Holiday's a relative term.' He grinned, wondering if he could tease her a little. 'And Maggie told me the other day that she found dedication very attractive in a man.'

Andrea smirked, leaning towards him. 'Yeah, she mentioned that to me, too. I don't want to burst your bubble, but I think she's referring to Joe.'

Laughing out loud with her was so very easy, so natural, and it helped lift the remains of the tension that was still pressing on his chest.

'I thought as much. Although I'm suitably

crushed.' He ventured another observation. 'Dedication's one thing, though. Putting together the procedures and training that make a rescue operation go as smoothly as this one is *really* impressive.'

He only needed to glance at Andrea to get the answer he was looking for. Her awkward smile betrayed her, showing that the slick organisation and thorough training of everyone involved was probably her doing.

'I'm guessing that you had a hand in that...?' When she didn't answer, he pressed a little further.

'The doctor who was here last wasn't very proactive. If there was an accident on the slopes, he'd step back and let the mountain-rescue team and the air-ambulance crews deal with it. I felt that there was a bit more that we could do in the time it took for those specialists to get here.'

Cal nodded. 'I think Giulia should be grateful that's your approach. It worked well.' No time had been lost in sending Giulia down to the hospital. She'd been brought off the slopes quickly and efficiently, so that she could be properly examined and prepared for the journey. Andrea's definition of a 'happy place' clearly didn't include just sitting back and going with the flow.

They strolled together from the helipad, taking the lift back downstairs. He saw Andrea wince slightly as she reached for the door of the surgery, and Cal reminded himself that she'd already brushed away his concern for her.

Suddenly he didn't care. He was on thin ice, skating dangerously close to shifting professional involvement onto a personal level. But she was hurt, and the only way he knew how to respond to that was with concern.

'Your shoulder's still bothering you?' He leaned forward, opening the door that led back into the clinic, and they both stood for a moment waiting for the other to go first. 'After you.'

Andrea grinned up at him. 'Nice manners. Dedication. No wonder Maggie's been getting all the wrong ideas.'

That sounded like a change of subject, which meant that her shoulder *was* still hurting. Andrea was heading towards the other treatment room, where Tomas was with the other snowboarder, and she didn't seem inclined to look back. That was okay. He could wait.

CHAPTER FOUR

CAL WAS GETTING more and more difficult to handle. Andrea had just about managed to blind herself to the fact that, not only was he very handsome, but he also had that indefinable quality that turned good looks into touch-me-now sexiness. She couldn't *quite* blind herself completely, but she had it under control.

Then he'd added his smile into the equation. His rock-steady presence, which had kept her focussed on the search for Giulia and not on the pain of the past. They'd worked well together, and Cal seemed to understand all her strengths and weaknesses.

No one could be expected to hold out against all that for long. And then Andrea remembered why she was here. Why she'd run away from everything and made a life up here in the mountains. Her happy place. Or, at least, the place where she could find a little peace.

Then Cal added one more entry to the list

of things that recommended him. When she arrived back in the main treatment room, everything was spick and span, the mess of emergency medical treatment all cleared away.

'I thought you would have gone by now...'

'I was waiting to see whether you were going to give me an answer to my question about your shoulder. And to see how Tomas's patient was doing.'

Cal's easy-going manner and his smile made his words sound less confrontational than they might have done. All the same, she ignored the first question in favour of the second.

'He's fine. He had a lucky escape. He was thrown clear and he's just got a few bruises.'

'I expect he's pretty worried about Giulia.'

Andrea twisted the corners of her mouth down. 'I told him she was on her way to the hospital and that she'd be well looked after there. He wasn't too concerned about that; he only met her last night. They had a few drinks together and he persuaded her to meet up with him again this morning for snowboarding.'

'Ah. So he won't be visiting her at the hospital, then.'

'I wouldn't imagine so. I'll wait here for her friends to get back, and I'll go down with them to the hospital if they want me to.'

'After you've done something about your shoulder, eh?'

His concern was chipping away at her defences. And the hint of male assertiveness was more than a little attractive. Andrea frowned at him and he pulled a face, frowning back.

'I saw how much it was hurting you. We could spend a moment exploring why you think that kind of pain should be ignored, if you like.'

'Or we could just get on and ignore it, without making so much fuss.' Andrea jutted her chin out at him.

'Yeah, we could do that. I'm not going to insult your intelligence by pretending to think that's okay...'

Please! Could he please just do *something* that made him seem less perfect? Just the once would be fine.

'I dislocated my shoulder in a car accident. It didn't heal well, and I had surgery to stabilise the joint last year. Sometimes it hurts a little...' Andrea lapsed into silence as he leaned back against the counter top, folding his arms. He was giving her the 'don't be a hero' look that she reserved for her most stubborn patients.

'All right, then.' She walked over to the treatment couch, sitting down on it. 'It *does* hurt. And I'd be grateful if you could take a look at it.'

He nodded quietly, clearly not feeling the need for an 'I told you so'. One more thing to like about him. Turning towards the sink, he started to wash his hands while Andrea pulled her sweater over her head.

'Ow!' Raising her arm hurt a great deal more than she'd thought it would. She heard his footsteps, and then felt his hand, gently steadying her arm.

'Just relax, would you…?'

There wasn't much choice. And relaxing against Cal, as he carefully disentangled her from the folds of her sweater, felt good. Great, even. His clean scent seemed to curl around her in remembrance of the pleasure that being close to someone could afford. Andrea pulled at the hook-and-loop fastening of her shoulder support, thankful that she'd worn a sleeveless vest underneath for extra warmth.

He didn't meet her gaze. Laying the sweater down next to her, he walked around the couch to adjust it to the right height for him to ex-amine her shoulder properly. Then she felt his fingers, tender on her skin.

'Anterior dislocation…?'

He must be able to see that from the scars,

one blotched and ragged from the accident, and a thinner, straighter one from the surgery.

'Ten out of ten.' She heard the sarcasm in her tone—one last-ditch attempt to resist the things she didn't want to feel. 'Sorry. Doctors make the worst patients...'

'So I've been told.' He chuckled quietly.

She felt his fingers, light on her shoulder. Andrea squeezed her eyes shut, trying not to think about his scent and the warmth of his body against hers. *He* wasn't aware of all that; he was entirely focussed on the task in hand.

'Have you seen all you need to see?' She couldn't stand much more of this. She was either going to turn and embrace him, or slap him away, and the second felt like a much safer option than the first.

'You must be a really great doctor, because you're a terrible patient.' He didn't seem in the slightest bit fazed by the sharpness in Andrea's tone. 'Give me another moment. When did you have the op?'

Andrea puffed out a sigh. Cal was actually trying to help her, and she shouldn't be so confrontational with him.

'Just over a year ago. The accident was two years before that but my shoulder never healed properly. It slipped out again while we were doing a rescue practice, and I went home last summer and had it fixed.'

'Looks as if it's healed well; it feels stable.' His fingers closed around her arm and Andrea concentrated on not resisting him as he flexed her shoulder, testing the movement. 'It's a little stiff. Been doing your exercises?'

'I've been a little busy. With the wedding.'

'Right.'

Andrea waited for him to say that was a poor excuse. Or that keeping her exercises up, even after her shoulder seemed fully healed, was important. Since he obviously wasn't going to, she might as well say it herself.

'I know. They only take twenty minutes...'

'Yeah.'

'I'll make sure I start doing them again.'

'Yep. Some anti-inflammatories and a week or so spent building your exercises back up again will do wonders. But you know that already.'

'Yes, I do.' Andrea twisted around, to face him. 'Hearing it doesn't go amiss though, so... thanks.'

'No problem. Consider me available to tell you what you already know at any time.' He bent to press the controls on the examination couch, lowering it until her feet touched the floor, and then turned away quickly. Andrea reached for her sweater, pulling it back over her head.

He was staring out of the window at the mountains, hands in his pockets. The silence was worse than anything he could possibly say at the moment.

'Giulia's going to need a lot of help.' It wasn't clear whether Cal was talking to her, or himself. Since she was in the room, Andrea decided to answer.

'Yes, she is. The trauma of being buried and half suffocated...' Andrea shrugged, wincing as her shoulder complained at the movement. 'But she'll have that. The doctors at the hospital here are very experienced in dealing with avalanche survivors and they know she's going to have to do a lot of talking.'

He turned, his gaze searching her face. 'Did you talk...about your accident?'

If he was jumping to conclusions, then his instincts were unerring. Or maybe he just looked a little closer than most people did, and saw the things that Andrea tried to hide. She took a deep breath.

'Yeah, they... It didn't help much, to be honest.' She'd been through everything with her counsellor, and it had made her feel neither better nor worse. Nothing had been able to penetrate the guilt and despair.

'Perhaps you just weren't ready.'

'Maybe. It's behind me now.' Andrea felt her lip quiver. Time hadn't blurred anything. Pulling Judd from the car and finding he was so badly injured that she couldn't save him was just as clear as it had always been.

'If talking will help you commit to your recovery a little better…'

Andrea caught her breath. Not Cal. He was the last person she could ever talk to about it. And he seemed to know that.

'You should find someone. It doesn't matter who, just someone who'll listen.'

The distance between them grew suddenly. It was the same distance she'd felt with anyone who tried to reach her and talk about the accident.

'I'll bear that in mind. Don't confuse letting things slip a bit because I'm busy with the wedding, with being in denial, Cal.'

His gaze seemed to bore into her. 'No. I won't do that.'

He saw right through her. And he knew that there was nothing more to say. Cal caught up his coat and left the room, closing the door quietly behind him.

Andrea didn't see him at lunchtime, and she didn't want to. She'd careened, out of control, between rage and the suspicion that Cal was right. Conjured his ghost up out of thin air, and asked what gave him the right to think he knew her, and then tearfully acknowledged that he was right, but that she didn't want to admit it. It seemed that Cal had the ability to get under her skin, even when he wasn't around.

But she could ignore all of that for the time being. News of the avalanche had spread around the hotel, and the manager was available in the lobby for anyone who needed reassurance. It was always important to take heed of the warning flags, but beyond that the slopes were safe. The snow patrol were checking them this afternoon, and the usual precautions were in place.

She called the hospital and got the good news that Giulia's scans had shown her back and head were uninjured. She had a fractured ankle, but she was recovering well from her ordeal. Then Andrea made the difficult call to Giulia's parents, adding her reassurances to those they'd already received, and telling them that someone from the hotel would meet them at the airport tomorrow morning. She'd go and see Giulia this afternoon, and call them again with an update.

Giulia's friends all wanted to visit her, and Andrea's suggestion that just two of them at her bedside was enough prompted a frenzied process of deciding who should go and who should stay behind. Finally, the decision was made, and they set off, Sylvia and Maria carrying presents and a card that had been signed by all of the group of friends. The half-hour journey on the funicular railway was followed by an hour's taxi ride, but finally they got there and found their way to Giulia's room.

'Would you like to wait here?' Andrea stopped at the door. 'I'll go in and see how she is first, eh?'

The two girls nodded. They'd started off in high spirits, but as they'd neared the hospital Sylvia had asked whether they should mention anything to Giulia about the accident. Andrea had told them that they should allow Giulia to talk, if and when she wanted to, but both girls seemed a little overwhelmed and afraid of saying the wrong thing.

But the first thing Andrea heard when she opened the door was the sound of quiet laughter. She stopped short in the doorway and saw Cal sitting by Giulia's bedside. He'd obviously been trying to supplement his schoolboy Italian with gestures and Giulia was smiling at his attempts to make himself understood.

'Oh...' Cal's hands fell to his lap. 'Sorry.

They said it was all right for me to come and see Giulia.'

And he'd made her smile. That alone made Andrea want to forgive him for everything.

'Don't be sorry. It's good of you to come.' Andrea could feel Sylvia and Maria jostling behind her, wanting to see what was going on. 'How are you getting on?'

'Not very well. I don't understand much of what she's saying…' Cal flashed Giulia a smile. *That* she understood. Who wouldn't understand one of Cal's smiles?

'Tell him…' Giulia turned her head towards Andrea, speaking in Italian. 'Tell him I like the flowers. And…thank you.'

Andrea nodded, relaying the message to Cal. He smiled at Giulia, stretching out his hand, and Giulia gripped it tightly. She remembered. Cal's hand, reaching for her. Letting her know that she'd been found.

'Tell her it was my pleasure. Any time.'

Andrea didn't need to translate. She had a feeling that Giulia already knew that.

Sylvia and Maria pushed past her into the room, and sat down quietly next to the bed. They seemed almost afraid to speak to Giulia, and Cal leaned over, gesturing to the large bag that Sylvia carried.

That message got through as well. Sylvia

opened the bag and produced a cuddly toy that had been bought from the hotel shop. She passed it over to Giulia, who hugged it, and soon the girls were talking animatedly. Cal slipped from his seat, joining Andrea in the doorway.

'Perhaps we should leave them to it. Fancy a cup of tea?'

'Yes, I do. You stay here though. I'll go and fetch some drinks.'

'Me? Stay here with three teenagers when I don't understand a word they're saying?' Cal shot her a pained look. 'Is this a subtle form of revenge?'

It might have been a few hours ago. But Andrea had seen the confidence in Giulia's face, and knew that Cal's presence had reassured her.

'I'd like to think I'd be far more imaginative if I wanted to take revenge on you.' Andrea smirked at him. 'Giulia's been talking to you?'

'Yes. I think she was talking about the avalanche, but I didn't understand what she was saying.' Cal rubbed thoughtfully at the back of his neck. 'Maybe that was the point.'

'I think it probably was. Just stay here with them and let them talk between themselves. I'll be back soon.' Andrea leaned a little closer, grinning up at him. 'Someone reminded me recently that talking's good. It seems that Giulia feels safe with you and able to talk.'

He pursed his lips. 'Okay. Point taken. Although she could have chosen more wisely. I'm a surgeon; my patients don't generally answer back.'

'Then I'm sure it'll be a learning exercise for you.' Andrea doubted it would be. Cal was so easy to talk to.

He frowned suddenly. 'I know my limitations. Ask Joe...'

That sounded suspiciously like a warning. One that was aimed at her. 'What if I ask you?'

His brow furrowed. Cal was clearly thinking carefully about his answer.

'I'd say I was a control freak. Uncompromising, when I'm not being inflexible.'

It *was* a warning. One that Andrea didn't understand, because it didn't sound like Cal at all. She shivered, wondering why he should think that of himself. And why he should be so keen to tell her about it.

'Just do it, Cal. I'll be back in a minute.'

He nodded quietly, turning towards the girls. Sylvia and Maria made room for him at Giulia's bedside and suddenly he was all charm again, smiling at Giulia and resuming his attempts at communication with a few words in halting Italian, supplemented by gestures and laughter.

Maybe she should take him at his word. Maybe she should stop thinking of him as the one person who might pull her back from her past, and allow her to look forward again. Or maybe she was already in too deep to take heed of any of Cal's warnings.

Cal wasn't sure what this was. In less than three days, he'd found himself caring about Andrea. As a friend, maybe. Perhaps as someone who seemed wounded, and who was crying out for a little honesty. Anything more was going somewhere he couldn't bring himself to think about.

But staying on, instead of leaving to go back to the hotel alone, was for Giulia's benefit. A sign that whatever she'd said to him, when she'd hung onto his hand, tears rolling down her cheeks, was okay. If Giulia had needed a safe place to express her fears, before she could begin the long process of letting go of them, then maybe that was what Andrea needed too.

But Cal knew that he wasn't the one. She should talk to a professional, or to Maggie, the friend she'd known since she was a child. Not him, because he couldn't maintain his distance from Andrea, however hard he tried.

And Mary had already told him that he was bad news for any woman to become involved with.

They left Giulia, drowsy and ready to sleep, all squeezing into a taxi parked outside the hospital. Sylvia and Maria met their friends at the railway terminus, leaving Cal and Andrea on the platform, waiting for the train to return back down the mountain again.

'Is it just me?' Cal watched the girls walk away. 'I want to give them a good talking-to about staying safe this evening. Not talking to strangers and getting back to the hotel before midnight.'

Andrea looked up at him. 'No, it's not just you. But they're eighteen, and they're perfectly sensible. They'll be fine, and anyway the last train leaves at eleven o'clock.'

'Do they know that?'

'Yes, of course they do. When I was eighteen I was...' She pressed her lips together suddenly.

'When you were eighteen you were what? Come on, you can't just stop there.'

'When I was eighteen, I was on my way to medical school, living on my own for the first time, getting to know new people and learning new things. What about you?'

'I was…probably doing much the same thing.'

'Probably? Don't you remember? I was so thrilled with it all. My dad took me to the bookshop, and we bought all of the books I'd need for my first term. Along with a few extra that he reckoned would come in handy. He's a doctor too.'

'So he and your mother were all for you going to medical school?' Cal wondered what that might be like. Two parents who agreed on something.

'Yes. Dad knew how hard the studying would be, but I could always go to him if I needed help with something. Mum was really pleased too.' Andrea pursed her lips. 'What about your parents?'

She seemed to know already that his experience had been different. It felt as if Andrea knew everything about him, without having to be told. 'My parents were…well, my father wasn't around when I left home for university. He travelled with his job a great deal.'

'What did he do?'

'He still does it, even though he should be thinking about retiring soon. I'm not sure he ever will, though. He's a news photographer— did you see the photos of the recent typhoon in Indonesia?'

Andrea's eyes widened. 'Your father's Terry Lewis? Yes, I saw the photos; they were incredible. Although, I wondered how anyone could manage to get so close...'

'Yeah, that was my first thought too. I've stopped worrying about him, because he'll never change. He always comes back in one piece, and before long he goes away again.' Cal could hear the bitterness in his voice.

'That must be very hard for your mother.'

'She doesn't read the news. Doesn't ever look at the pictures. He and Mum divorced when I was ten. She couldn't cope with him never being there. Or worrying about what he was up to.'

Andrea nodded. The wind whipped along the station platform, bringing with it flurries of snow, and she shivered, stamping her feet. Cal tucked his hand in the crook of her arm, guiding her towards the waiting room, and she walked over to the small heater in the corner.

'That's better.' She stripped off her gloves, holding her hands out to the warmth. 'So your parents didn't approve of you going to medical school, then?'

'It's not that they didn't approve. It just wasn't what either of them had decided I should be doing with my life. Mum wanted me to do something that guaranteed my staying in one place and settling down. My father wanted similar guarantees that I'd be travelling the world, the way he does.'

'That's what you do, isn't it?'

'Not quite in the way he wanted me to. I travel to help set up medical facilities in the places that need them most. He travels for kicks, goes to the most dangerous places he can find. He doesn't think that's the same.'

'And what about your mother?'

This had already gone further than Cal had meant it to, but he didn't want to turn back, now. 'My mother lives with it. She knows I don't take the kinds of risks that my father does, but she still asks me whether I'm any nearer to settling down whenever she sees me.'

Andrea's fingers curled, as if she were trying to get hold of something. Trying to think it all through. That was what Cal had been doing for most of his life, and he could have told her that it was an insoluble conundrum.

'I suppose…it must be hard, finding your own space when they both had such different ambitions for you.'

That was just how he'd felt when he was eighteen. Suffocated by his parents' ambitions. 'Yeah. It was. It took the gloss off things, knowing that there was never anything I could do that would make them both proud of me.'

'Is that what you meant when you said you were inflexible? It strikes me that everyone should be a little inflexible when it comes to fulfilling what they want to do with their lives. You should be proud of yourself.'

The look in her eyes did make Cal feel proud—that he could engender such warmth, such compassion.

'It is what it is. My job... I feel that's what I'm meant to be doing.' Cal held his shaking hands out to the warmth of the heater. It suddenly meant a great deal, more than he'd bargained for, that someone understood. It meant a great deal more that it wasn't just any old someone, but that Andrea understood.

'That's nice. It's a good thing.' Andrea seemed lost in her thoughts again. Cal wondered what she had been meant to do, feeling sure that, whatever it was, it wasn't to be a hotel doctor at a mountain resort. She'd seemed to thrive on her work today, but it was just one day, in a whole procession of days that brought the same minor injuries and illnesses, which in truth could have been treated by any competent year one medical student.

The train drew into the station, and people spilled out of it, ready for their evening out. Andrea suddenly caught his hand, hurrying out of the waiting room.

'Quick…' She was weaving through the crowd, towards the back of the train, right at the other end of the platform. When she got to the last carriage, they jumped inside, just as the doors were closing.

'This is the carriage that suits you?' It was good to forget about everything that the past held, and just run towards something. Cal wondered if Andrea had some aim in mind, or whether she'd just wanted to run.

'Yes, this is the one. It's my favourite part of the train.' The carriage was deserted, most people wanting to go out at this time, rather than back to the hotel. She led him to the end, pulling back the sliding glass doors and entering a domed glass section.

He already knew that the views were spectacular, but as the train pulled away from the station he realised that being surrounded entirely by glass was a different experience entirely. Cal took hold of the handrail to steady himself, feeling almost as if he were suspended in mid-air as the funicular climbed away from the town, and up into the mountains.

It was breathtaking. The snow-covered peaks sparkled in the setting sun, a clear sky above their heads. Beneath them, the lights of the village were drawing further and further away. It felt almost as if they were flying.

'What do you think?'

Cal smiled. 'You chose well. This is definitely the best carriage.'

The train lurched slightly, and he reached out to steady her. She turned, looking up at him, and Cal couldn't draw away.

'This inflexible, uncompromising control-freakery of yours...'

So she'd taken note of what he'd said. It was almost a disappointment. But Cal couldn't help the sizzling tension that flashed between them, and it had seemed only fair to give her a reason to ignore it.

'You don't believe me?' Mary hadn't believed him, and that had caused all kinds of pain...for both of them.

'I believe you. I'm just wondering if you're as good at it as you make out.'

There was no answer to that. Suddenly the world seemed to be turning around them both in a giddying whirlpool. Here, at the centre, was the only thing that mattered.

And here he could entertain the thought that Andrea might be right. That he could change, and that she could change and... Suddenly she moved against him, standing on her toes and planting a kiss on his cheek.

'What...?' He didn't dare ask what she was doing.

'You see, if you really were in control, I wouldn't have been able to surprise you like that.'

Was that a challenge? Some kind of battle of wills? He wasn't in control and they both knew it. Maybe Andrea wanted him to say it.

He drew back a little, gazing into her eyes. Such gorgeous eyes, that set the ever-changing beauty of the mountains to shame. Touching her cheek with his fingertips was like feeling the warmth of a summer's day trickling through his senses.

'Maybe I've just met my match…'

'Maybe you have.'

She brushed a kiss against his lips. When Cal returned it, she smiled up at him.

He couldn't resist kissing her again, and this time she responded more urgently. As if this one moment were everything, and she was going to wring every last drop of its potential from it.

It *was* everything. It had to be, because it couldn't be repeated. The thought only made Cal more determined, desperately seeking everything that he knew wouldn't happen again. He felt her shift in his arms, clinging to him tightly. The feeling was electrifying.

'This isn't what we agreed…' He had to stop

this. 'We can pretend all we like, but neither of us is in the right place for a relationship.'

'I know.' Her eyes seemed almost luminous in the light of a brilliant sunset. 'Maybe we could pretend just a little more.'

He could keep this pretence up for a very long time. When she kissed him again, it was just as wonderful as the first touch of her lips—more so, because he was already under her spell. Already bound to her in a way that defied logic.

'I'd say that was pretty near perfect.'

Cal raised his eyebrows. 'Pretty near? What's your definition of perfect?'

'Trying it one more time...'

CHAPTER FIVE

WHAT ON EARTH had she been thinking? Ah, yes. That was right. She *hadn't* been thinking.

But Andrea hadn't been able to resist it. He seemed somehow as broken as she was, and she'd wanted to push him the way he'd pushed her. To make him see that his future didn't need to be defined by his past, in the same way that his strength had made her believe that maybe, one day, she'd spread her wings and fly again.

And…she'd just wanted to kiss him. To see whether it would be as perfect as she'd imagined. And he'd gone and surprised her, by making it so much more than she could ever have dreamed.

It had been rash, and exciting, and Cal probably was a bit of a control freak after all. But in the nicest way possible because he still made her feel as if she were the most beautiful woman alive.

But it *was* just an interlude. As they drew into the hotel terminus, the tender regret in his face told her that Cal wasn't taking this any further. Maybe he was right. He'd struggled so hard to stand in his own space, and he needed someone who could stand with him. Being a part of Cal's life would mean stepping out of her own comfort zone, her happy place where she didn't have to think about letting down someone she loved, ever again. If she really cared about him, she would let him go.

They stepped off the train, and the doors slid closed behind them. Andrea was wondering just how much of a goodbye this was when he held out his arm, a wry smile on his face.

'You're still speaking to me, then?' She slipped her hand into the crook of his elbow.

He shot her a questioning look. 'Always. I'm always speaking to you, Andrea.'

That was the nice thing about Cal. He said what was on his mind, and expected her to do the same.

'That's good. I'm glad about that.'

He nodded. 'What happens on the train, stays on the train?'

If that was the case, she could spend the whole of the next week riding up and down on the funicular railway. Andrea resisted the temptation to suggest it. They had a wedding to organise.

'Yes. As long as we can still be friends.'

'I'd like that very much.'

They walked together into the hotel lobby. It felt wrong to leave him here when the night could hold so much more for them, but it was the only right thing to do.

'I promised to ring Giulia's parents when I got back, to let them know how she is. They'll be here in the morning…'

Cal nodded. 'That's good. Will you be free later on, to go through some of the arrangements for the wedding?'

'I was hoping you might say that. Yes, after my morning surgery?'

'I'll meet you then.'

Cal hesitated, smiling suddenly. 'I think too much of you to kiss you goodnight. It doesn't mean I don't want to.'

He turned, walking away without looking back, as if he knew that Andrea was watching him go. He was a lot braver than she was. A lot stronger. And he was willing to give up the idea of a brief affair, in order to be her friend. There was something chivalrous about that, and the thought warmed her as she walked back up to her apartment alone.

* * *

Andrea found Cal waiting for her after her morning surgery the following day with a long list of questions. What would happen if someone was taken ill at the wedding? Did the translator, required at all Italian weddings, need to be licensed, or would someone who spoke both Italian and English do? Could the three other bridesmaids, ranging in age from six to ten, be persuaded not to fidget during the ceremony?

'I'm not entirely sure that's going to be possible.' The earnest look on his face made Andrea smile. 'Anyway, fidgeting and pulling faces is half the charm of it. I'll be stopping them from doing anything really disruptive.'

'Okay.' He seemed to be mentally scanning the long list of disruptive things that little girls could do. 'I'll leave the exact definition of disruptive for you to work out. What about the venue?'

'You haven't seen it?'

He shook his head. 'Not yet. Just your photographs.'

Cal really was leaving nothing to chance. Andrea led him to the hall at the back of the building, unlocking the double doors with the key card that hung around her neck.

'So wheelchair access isn't going to be a problem.' He stepped inside, looking around.

The large empty space had been designed to take advantage of its surroundings. The floor-to-ceiling windows and a domed glass roof made it seem as if they could almost touch the gentle slope that lay between them and the mountains.

'Spectacular.' Cal walked to the centre of the space. 'You're going to decorate in here?'

'I suggested that Maggie kept it simple, with just some flowers along the aisle we'll create between the seating and two large arrangements at the front. I'm not entirely sure that anything we can contrive will compete with this. There are floodlights outside that make the most of the scenery after dark.' She gestured towards the windows.

Cal nodded his approval. 'And then we all go through to the reception.'

'Yes, there's a lobby at the other end of this space, which leads straight through to the large ballroom, where there will be a sit-down meal and then dancing later on. This space will be cleared and Maggie and Joe will come back in here to cut the cake around about sunset, so we'd better hope it's a good one on the day...'

A lump formed in her throat, at the thought of

the use that she and Cal had made of yesterday's sunset.

She saw a knowing glimmer in Cal's eyes. He felt it too. However hard they both tried to deny it, Maggie had been right. There was something between her and Cal that couldn't be quantified but was as solid and real as the mountains that surrounded them.

'That sounds very romantic.' He was clearly making an effort to keep from smiling. 'You've thought of everything.'

'The hotel hosts weddings on a regular basis so I've had the opportunity to see what other people have done, and learn from it.'

'Now that you mention learning from experience, I've been thinking about all you've done here, at the hotel's medical suite. I'd really like to take a look around. Professional interest…'

That was a little more daunting than wedding arrangements. Andrea didn't talk about what had happened before she came here, but she'd used the experience she'd gained, working quietly to make small changes, which all added up to big ones. The medical centre was working smoothly and efficiently now, and no one even noticed the lack of fuss over things that had once been dramas.

Of course, Cal had noticed. It was part of

his job. And it was perfectly natural that he should take an interest.

'Of course. I'll show you around some time.'

'How about now? I think we're just about done here, aren't we?'

He wasn't going to let her off the hook. That was a challenge, because she knew that Cal would question her, and he'd already shown that he took nothing for granted. But her heart was beating a little faster at the opportunity to show someone who really knew all of the issues involved in what she'd done here.

He followed her to the medical centre, and she opened the door.

'Waiting room.'

Cal was grinning as he looked around the bright comfortable space.

'Very nice. Did you make any changes here?'

Andrea rolled her eyes. He knew as well as she did that every part of the doctor-patient process had to be thought through.

'Actually, I did. The old doctor used to have a drop-in area here, where people could get leaflets and over-the-counter medicines and dressings. It was convenient and very popular—you'd be surprised how many people would rather treat themselves than have a doctor disrupt their holiday by telling them they're ill. So now everyone has to at least see me or Tomas, and we dispense the medicines free.'

Cal nodded. 'I imagine that's a particular issue with some of the hardcore skiers.'

'Yes. I had a guy who sauntered in the other week, five minutes before the end of my surgery, wondering if I had a couple of paracetamol to spare. It turned out he had a fractured wrist but he wasn't going to let a little thing like that keep him from the slopes.'

'I wouldn't think he was too happy about you sending him down to the hospital.'

'I dealt with it here. And he actually didn't mind all that much; it's sometimes just a matter of saving people's pride. He was here with his mates, and he didn't want to be the one to say that he couldn't do anything, so I said it for him.'

'You can deal with fractures here?'

'Simple ones, yes. We have X-ray facilities, which were never used before I got here… You want to see?' Andrea was beginning to feel that she wanted Cal's assessing eye to see what she'd done here. His approval was addictive, and she was beginning to crave it.

'Yes, very much…'

Andrea didn't make a big thing of it, but the medical centre here was well organised and able to deal with a wide range of medical situations. She'd anticipated various different scenarios, working out the best way to deal with each of them. He was very well aware that this type of forward planning took experience.

'You've obviously done this kind of thing before.'

'Worked at a ski resort? No, this is my first time.' She deliberately ducked the question.

Cal wished he could show her that he wasn't fooled by this. Not just because he wanted to know all about Andrea, but because it felt as if there was something there that was just bursting to get out—a committed, talented doctor, who knew exactly how to manage a medical project on her own, and who had the ability to take any situation and make it better. But he'd already gone too far down that route, and Andrea had as much as told him to mind his own business.

'Your job must involve a great deal of contingency planning.' She switched the subject adroitly onto him.

'Yes, it does. A lot of the places I visit have a great deal of potential, and it's just a matter of providing a few things that will help it come to fruition. They tell me what they need, and I do my best to provide it.'

'Not the other way round?' From the smile

she gave him, Andrea already knew the answer she wanted to hear.

'No. Projects that we help with are led by local communities and experts. We listen and discuss, and offer what resources we can. That might be money, or it might be training or scholarships. In my experience it's very rarely telling someone what I think they need.'

She nodded. Right answer. 'And your surgical skills?'

'I've learned a lot more than I've been able to teach. I may be able to help with the more complex surgical procedures and techniques, made possible by technology that's hard to obtain in developing countries, but I'm constantly surprised by how much is possible with so little.'

Right answer again. Cal's suspicions were fast solidifying into certainty. Andrea had once worked on projects far beyond the scope of her work here. Something bad had happened, and she'd been hurt. She'd found her 'happy place' here, but she couldn't quite leave behind the impulse to make a difference.

And maybe that was his way in. 'I've got some photos. Rather a lot of them, actually.'

'Oh! On there?' She pointed to the tablet he was holding.

'Yes. Would you like a bite to eat?'

'That sounds good. If you have the time...'

He had nothing else to do. These two weeks had been earmarked for Maggie and Joe, and now they were for Andrea too.

'How about pizza?'

Everyone seemed to know Andrea. As she walked past the tables in the pizzeria, there were flashed smiles and greetings from both holidaymakers and staff. But she didn't appear to have any real friends. She was clearly popular amongst the staff, but not really one of them. And the ever-changing tide of hotel guests meant that they were never any more than just passing acquaintances.

She found a table by the window and sat down. Cal decided to try something. His photographs were ordered by country, and he slid the tablet across the table towards her, allowing Andrea to choose which she looked at first. Maybe that would tell him where she'd been.

India. She flipped through the photographs, asking questions and stopping to study some carefully. It wasn't India.

South America. Andrea spent a little more time over his photographs from Peru, but that was just because this batch included some he'd taken of one of the mobile operating theatres that the clinic sponsored. It was no particular surprise that Andrea wanted to know more about that. So, it wasn't South America.

Then their pizzas arrived. She laid his tablet aside, and they both started to eat.

'Your photos are amazing. You have a good eye.'

'My father taught me. He always says that photography is a dialogue.'

Andrea shot him a mystified look. 'That sounds pretty deep to me.'

'Yeah, it does to most people.' Most people didn't admit it and just nodded sagely, but Andrea's enquiring mind wouldn't let it go. 'He means that photography is all about how you interact with what's around you. What you pick out as important and how you choose to show it.'

'Bit difficult to interact with a tornado, I'd say.' Andrea smirked at him.

No one had ever really questioned that because Terry Lewis was acclaimed as one of the best photographers of his generation. No one but Andrea, who weighed everything up, and came to her own conclusions.

'I think it's a conversation with himself. He's drawn to the excitement; he feels most alive when he's facing something with such raw power.'

Andrea turned the corners of her mouth

down, but said nothing. It came as a relief that she didn't try to convince him that the quality of his father's photographs justified everything, because she knew as well as he did that it didn't. They were both doctors, and their challenges were in putting pieces back together again, not tearing them apart.

She abandoned her knife and fork, picking up a slice of her pizza so she could eat and flip through the photographs at the same time. The ones of New Guinea prompted questions about the particular challenges that the region faced, and those of Malaysia about the children's hospital he'd visited. Unless there was some sign of recognition that he'd missed, the world of possibilities was beginning to shrink.

'Oh! These are wonderful.' She abandoned the last slice of pizza so that she could pay full attention to the photographs in front of her. If photography *was* a dialogue, then the emotion in her eyes said everything.

Africa. It was Africa.

There was no need to ask, and maybe Andrea would have evaded his question anyway or told him to mind his own business. He watched as she flipped slowly through the images, returning the smiles of the hospital staff and patients he'd photographed. Then she put the tablet aside, decisively switching it off.

'Tell me you've brought your camera with you.' Cal had seen a flicker of regret when Andrea put the tablet to one side, but now she was smiling at him.

'Yeah. I've been taking a few shots. When no one's looking.'

'They're the best kind.' She leaned conspiratorially across the table towards him. 'And speaking of photographs, I've been putting off doing Joe and Maggie's album for too long now. Have you sorted out the ones you have of Joe yet?'

'No, not yet. I've been wondering how embarrassing I can go…'

She grinned naughtily. 'I'd say somewhere between uncomfortable and completely mortifying would be about right.'

'Okay. I'll get right on it. What are you up to tomorrow? I need to take a look at the venues you suggested for Joe's stag, but I should be back in the evening. I really should have dinner with Maggie and Joe tonight; I've hardly seen them since we arrived.'

'Tomorrow's good. I can come along with you in the afternoon if you'd like. I'll ask Tomas if he'll fill in for me at the surgery. I'm due some time off, and he's happy to do it while I concentrate on the wedding.'

'Sounds great. I'll come and find you after

your morning surgery, and maybe we can get some lunch in the village.'

She nodded, inspecting the discarded slice of pizza on her plate. 'I think that's cold, now. Shall we have some dessert?'

'I'll just have coffee. But don't let me stop you.' Cal handed her the menu, and she started to peruse it, pressing her lips together as if this was a real treat and she should choose carefully.

As beautiful as she was, however much joy she took from little things, it still felt as if there was something missing. Some piece of her that she'd deliberately pushed aside in exchange for a fragile peace of mind. He knew now that Africa had once been her dream and she never talked about it.

Cal dismissed the thought. Maybe it was better to forget all about it and concentrate on the wedding. But regardless of whether he was her friend, or her lover, he owed Andrea more than that now. And he was determined to pay that debt.

CHAPTER SIX

THE NEXT DAY was bright and clear, a cold wind blowing in from the mountains. Andrea stumbled out of bed, still bleary eyed from a dream that found her shivering in Cal's arms, sheltering from a blast of freezing air. She'd woken to find that the duvet had slipped halfway off the bed during the night. That accounted for the cold part of the dream, but not for the warmth of his touch.

She should never have kissed him. She'd given in to temptation and the exhilaration of the moment, but this was the second night now that she'd dreamed about him. And the second morning that she'd woken with the feeling that after everything they'd done in those dreams, she couldn't look him in the eye.

A shower and a glance at her wedding folder over breakfast would handle it. Focus on what needed to be done.

The morning's list of patients included a

strained back and two upset stomachs, along with the usual cuts and bruises. Somehow it didn't seem enough. Those photographs of Cal's had awoken a longing that she'd thought she'd managed to put behind her. It was yet another thing that she needed to ignore if she was going to get through the run-up to the wedding in one piece.

She got to the reception area bang on twelve, but he was already waiting for her, sitting in one of the deep armchairs and reading the paper. When he saw her, he refolded the paper, putting it back into the rack, and grabbed his coat and scarf.

'It looks cold out there.' He was dressed for it, wearing a thick sweater that emphasised the breadth of his shoulders. She allowed herself to watch as he pulled on his coat, because watching Cal do pretty much anything was a pleasure.

The manager interrupted her reverie, and Andrea swallowed down the impulse to tell her that she was busy and to go away.

'Andrea, we've got a situation.'

That was hotel-speak for something bad happening. 'What's the matter, Gina?'

'We have a missing child. His name's Matthew, he's ten years old, and the last time his parents saw him was half an hour ago. We're making a thorough search of the building and the outdoor teams are setting off.'

Andrea nodded. She'd helped write and implement the search procedures, and she knew it was unlikely that an in-house search would have missed the boy. She held the current record for being able to evade a co-ordinated search drill and it stood at twenty-four minutes.

'Does anyone know where he might have gone?'

'We fear he may be outside. His parents decided not to go out skiing because of the cold and apparently he was disappointed. And his coat is gone.'

That was one layer of warmth at least. But a ten-year-old, alone in the snow, in these wind-chill conditions, would get cold very fast.

'I've paged Tomas, as he's on duty this afternoon. But we can do with all the help we can get.' Gina knew already that Andrea wouldn't be going anywhere when there was a missing child that needed to be found.

'Of course.' Andrea turned to find Cal and bumped straight into him. He'd been standing right behind her, listening to what Gina had been saying.

'I'll help.' Clearly it wasn't necessary for

Andrea to apologise to him about cancelling their afternoon. Cal wasn't going anywhere either.

Gina turned to him, smiling. 'Thank you, but our staff have everything under control. We're advising all guests—'

'I'm a doctor. I've worked with search and rescue teams before.' Cal clearly wasn't going to take no for an answer.

Gina's smile turned from placatory to businesslike. 'In that case, thank you. Andrea will tell you where you're needed.'

The rescue plan stated that Andrea and Tomas would stay in the medical centre, so that they could be summoned quickly if they were needed. But a lost child required that as many people as possible should be out searching. If she was with Cal, then Andrea could risk expanding her role a little...

'I think the best thing is for Tomas to stay in the medical centre, so he's there to receive the boy when he's found. Cal and I will go outside to see if we can help the search teams there. You're co-ordinating, Gina?'

'Yes. You have your phone?' Gina would send text updates to all of the team leaders' phones. If the initial search proved fruitless, the Search and Rescue helicopters would be scrambled.

Andrea nodded, turning to Cal. 'We'll get going, then.'

The organisation was impressive. Ski lessons and other activities had quickly been called to a halt, and some of the guests were filing back towards the hotel, while others had volunteered to join the search teams, which were already beginning to spread out across pre-defined areas. Cal could see skidoos further out, making for high points and covering the ever-widening distance that a ten-year-old might have travelled.

Speed was of the essence, and every moment that Andrea had managed to shave from the staff's response times was another moment when the boy could be found safe and well.

Andrea stopped to speak to one of the hotel staff who was wearing a hi-vis jacket, and seemed to be co-ordinating the outdoor search teams. He handed her one of the small backpacks that lay ready at his feet, and Cal took it from her before she could shoulder it herself.

'He has a red jacket. We'll go up to the ridge, over there.' Andrea indicated a low ridge that ran to one side of one of the nursery slopes.

'Okay. It looks like a pretty stiff climb. Do you think he'll have made it up there?'

'It's possible; there's a way around the ridge from the hotel, which is a flatter walk. Or he might have climbed. There are other teams covering the more likely places, and from up there we'll get a bird's eye view.'

They set off at a brisk pace and as they reached the untrodden snow, Cal looked for footprints or any other signs that the boy had been this way. As the incline became steeper, he saw that Andrea was holding her left arm a little stiffly and decided to say nothing. Andrea probably wouldn't thank him for it, and it might just be an instinctive protectiveness of what she knew was a weakness. He'd deal with it if she seemed to be in any difficulty.

'This kind of thing happens a lot, then?' Perhaps he should revise his opinion of Andrea's job.

'We don't usually get one incident like this in a week, let alone two.' Andrea stopped to catch her breath. 'We have our share of lost kids, but generally by the time we've done a search inside they're found. And avalanches aren't that unusual anywhere in the Alps, but we patrol regularly and most people obey the warning flags.'

'So this is unusual.' Cal was scanning the ridge, looking for any sign of the boy.

'Very. You chose the wrong week if you were expecting a holiday.'

Her phone beeped and she pulled it from her pocket, reading the text that had just been received. 'They've finished the search inside the hotel. They're doing a second sweep, but I doubt they've missed him.'

'So he's probably out here somewhere.'

'Yep. And the sooner we find him, the better.' Andrea started walking again. It was hard going. The snow was deep in places and the wind seemed to be getting stronger, stinging his face. But Andrea's quiet determination told Cal that she wouldn't be stopping until the boy was found, however long that took.

When they reached the top of the ridge, Andrea dropped to her knees in the snow. This time Cal asked.

'Okay?' He tried to make the question sound casual.

'Yeah. That got my heart pumping...'

His too. Cal shot her a grin, and slipped the backpack from his shoulders, inspecting its contents. Basic medical supplies, distress flags and flares, a pair of binoculars... He took the binoculars out, scanning in a slow, three-hundred-and-sixty-degree arc.

'Anything?'

'No…' A movement caught his eye and Cal swung back to locate it. 'Over there. I'm not sure…'

As he handed her the binoculars, he saw a flash of red. Andrea followed the direction of his pointing finger and let out a cry.

'Yes. It's him. I can see him moving.'

That was something. Andrea pulled her phone from her pocket, stripping off her gloves and hitting autodial.

'Gina, we're at the top of the ridge. We can see him on the far side… Yeah, the snow ambulance is going to have to come round… Great, thanks.'

She ended the call, putting her phone back into her pocket. Cal had been surveying the steep drop on the other side of the ridge. Andrea was right in saying that the snow ambulance couldn't make it over the top of the ridge, but the flatter route would take longer. They needed to get to the boy as fast as they could.

A man could make it down there. Maybe… He took a moment to gauge the angle of the incline, reckoning that if he lost his footing at least the snow would break his fall.

'They're sending the snow ambulance now. I need you to stay here and guide it to Matthew; they might not be able to see him…'

'Where are you going?'

'I'm going to try to get to him.' Andrea started to survey the steep drop with the binoculars.

What? Not in a million years. Not even if her shoulder had been in perfect condition.

A bright, hard protectiveness flared in Cal's chest.

He wasn't going to argue with her. There wasn't any point, because there was no way that he'd let Andrea go down there. She was still looking through the binoculars and never even noticed him bending to take the flares from the backpack and leaving them in the snow at her feet. Then he shouldered the backpack, took one deep breath to steady himself and started to slide down towards the boy.

No! Cal!

The shock was almost as if she'd been punched in the chest. Cal was making his way down the steep incline, his stance almost that of a skier, leaning into the slope with his arms held out to keep his balance. She had no choice but to stay here now. She needed to use the flares he'd left behind to help to guide the snow ambulance.

Tears of helpless rage began to form in Andrea's eyes. She'd lost Judd. She'd watched him die, unable to save him. She couldn't lose Cal. Fixing her gaze on him, as if somehow that might improve his balance, she watched his progress.

Just as she thought he was going to make it, he fell, tumbling down the last ten feet of the drop. Andrea let out a howl of anguish, and then he moved. He got to his feet, brushing himself off, and then... *Then* he had the audacity to wave at her.

Fine. She wasn't waving back. She watched as Cal walked towards the tiny figure in the snow. There seemed to be hardly any reaction—Matthew must already be suffering from the effects of the cold. Cal bent down in front of him, taking the thermal blanket from the backpack and wrapping it around him. He picked Matthew up, carrying him to the meagre shelter of a rocky outcrop.

They were both safe, she had to concentrate on that. Andrea jumped as her phone rang. She had to blow on her fingers to warm them before the touch screen would register.

'I've got him. He's a little drowsy, but he's lucid. His feet are wet, and he has no gloves, but his body seems warm. Any idea when the snow ambulance will be here?'

'It shouldn't be any more than ten minutes.'
Andrea closed her eyes, counting to ten. She'd
give Cal a piece of her mind later.

'Great, thanks.'

Andrea ended the call, not trusting herself
to say any more. She called Gina, relaying the
boy's status, and then trained the binoculars
on the path that she knew the snow ambulance
would be taking. When she saw it, she let off
the flare. Cal would see it too, and know that
help was almost there.

She saw Cal make his way towards the vehicle as it drew up next to him. He could start
to warm Matthew up in the ambulance, and
Tomas would be waiting in the medical centre,
ready to shepherd them inside and take over
his treatment.

She started to trudge back down the slope.
Cal was all right; he'd taken a tumble but he'd
got back up again. She shouldn't care so much
that it was him who'd taken the risk of sliding
down to the boy, instead of her. But she did.

Andrea was back in time to see the ambulance
draw up, and Cal carry the boy into the medical centre. He handed him over to Tomas, just
as a woman burst through the door from the
waiting room, crying hysterically.

'You're the doctor…?' She caught hold of

Andrea's arm. 'I'm Matthew's mother. Please, is he all right?'

'I'm going to examine him now.' Andrea tried to break free, but Matthew's mother was holding her tight and a man, tight-lipped and white-faced with worry, was blocking Andrea's path through to the treatment room.

Then, suddenly all the obstacles melted away. Cal had freed Andrea, and managed to manoeuvre himself in between her and the couple, declaring himself to be a doctor, and able to tell them what was going on. It was best if they all waited together and gave Andrea a chance to examine Matthew properly.

It was the right thing to do. Normally any child would benefit from having their mother present during an examination, but Matthew's mother's tears would only distress him further. And Cal's quiet reassurances seemed to be calming both of Matthew's parents. Andrea shot them a smile, before hurrying after Tomas into the treatment room.

Cal had already stripped off Matthew's shoes and jeans, wrapping his legs in another blanket from the ambulance to keep him warm. Andrea examined his fingers and toes carefully, while Tomas turned the warm-air blowers on to warm him gently. His hands and feet were cold, and very red, but there was no sign of frostbite.

'Keep monitoring him, Tomas. I'll be out in the waiting room if you need me.' Andrea was pleased with what she saw, and it was time to go and see how Cal was doing with the boy's parents.

Matthew's mother was much calmer now, her husband sitting with his arm around her. Both were listening as Cal spoke quietly to them, his words inaudible, but his manner calm and reassuring.

He was so good at defusing situations, finding a way through with the minimum of fuss. Even Andrea felt the warmth of the atmosphere here in the waiting room, as she sat down next to him.

'I've examined Matthew and he's very cold, but I don't see any signs of frostbite. He has what we call frostnip, which is much less serious, and we can deal with that easily now that we have him in the warm.'

'May I see him?' Matthew's mother glanced at Cal and he smiled. He must have already told her that the best thing she could do for her son was to be calm.

'Of course. He's a little bit drowsy but that's to be expected. He's complaining that his hands are cold as well, but don't let that worry you. Feeling cold is a sign that there's no permanent damage.'

Matthew's father nodded. 'Cal said you'd be warming him up slowly.'

'Yes, that's right. It may take a little while, but you can sit with him. You might like to bring a few books or toys down, so that you can keep him amused when he starts to feel a bit better.'

'Thank you.' Matthew's mother turned, clasping Cal's hand between hers. 'And you too, Doctor. Thank you.'

Andrea ushered Matthew's parents into the treatment room, where Tomas had him tucked up under a blanket, his hands and feet protruding so that they'd warm gradually. She pulled a chair up, beside the couch, and Matthew's mother sat down, smiling at her son. Signalling to Tomas to stay put, she walked back out into the waiting room.

'He's okay?' Cal turned to her.

'Yes. We got to him in time.' Andrea pressed her lips together. She'd decided that she wouldn't mention Cal's precipitous slide down the slope.

'Good.'

She would have left it at that but Cal was watching her thoughtfully, the look on his face making it very clear he wasn't going to let things rest. She didn't want to let things rest either. Andrea took a moment to choose her words carefully.

'I wish you'd said what you were going to do. Before you went down that slope.'

'You were thinking that you wanted to discuss it?'

'In these situations it's always a good thing.' Andrea tried to keep the observation as neutral as possible.

'Yes, it is. And considering the impressive organisation that you've put in place for emergencies, I was a little surprised that you didn't discuss who was best placed to tackle that slope with me.'

Andrea frowned. It was difficult to work out whether that was a compliment or an insult. Or whether it was just the truth, which was rather more challenging at the moment.

'*I'm* extremely surprised that you didn't discuss it with *me*.' Andrea pressed her lips together. This was turning into one of those petty tit-for-tat arguments that generally didn't get anyone anywhere. But she was so cross with Cal…

'Would it have made any difference if I had?'

Andrea puffed out a breath. Of course it wouldn't. She'd decided to go herself, and nothing that Cal could have said would have changed her mind.

'Cal, I know you've got a lot of experience. But it may have slipped your mind that I'm actually on the payroll here as the doctor in charge.'

'Pulling rank on me isn't going to change the facts, Andrea. If you'd taken a fall like the one I did, I'd probably have you in the other treatment room practising my reduction technique on your shoulder.' Cal was obviously getting irritated too.

She couldn't help that. This couldn't go unanswered.

'I've had the surgery, Cal. My shoulder might hurt at times, but it's probably no more likely to dislocate than yours. And if you want to play doctors, let's do that, shall we? You're cold, you need to warm up a bit.'

Even though his manner had been one of relaxed well-being with Matthew's mother, he *was* shivering now. No wonder, he'd ripped his over-trousers in the fall, and his jeans were wet. And Andrea had noticed that he'd left his coat in the ambulance, so he must have taken it off and tucked it over Matthew to provide another layer of warmth.

'I'm fine.' He pressed his lips together. It

was a bit late now to decide he didn't want to talk about it.

'No, you're not, Cal. Will you please go and warm up and let me get on with my job?' At least he could negotiate whatever risks that the journey back to his room presented without Andrea having to stand and watch him.

He gave her a long, searching look. If he thought that would give her time to change her mind, then he could think again. As she'd watched him go down that slope, the truth had slapped her in the face. She cared too much about Cal. And now she felt ashamed that she'd reacted the way she had. This all had to stop.

'Okay. I dare say you'll be busy with Matthew for a while, but I'll see you later?' His voice had taken on those warm honey tones again, and only his eyes flashed a message of concern.

Already her resolve to keep him at a distance was weakening. Andrea got to her feet, and opened the door that led out of the medical suite. 'Yeah. Maybe. I'll see how things go.'

Cal went to his room. Andrea was the doctor here, and she had every right to order him out of her surgery. To be fair, she hadn't actually ordered him out, it just felt as if she had.

He stripped off his clothes. He *was* cold, and

red patches on his legs where his jeans had been wet were beginning to tingle painfully. That was all to the good; it showed he was beginning to warm up again and hadn't done himself any damage. He hadn't even noticed that he was cold before, he'd been so focussed on looking after Matthew and then talking with the parents.

But Andrea's cool reaction afterwards had frozen him to the bone. All of the things he'd wondered about were spinning in his head, along with the knowledge that he too could have handled things a little better. He pulled on a pair of warm sweatpants, and a T-shirt, adding a sweater for good measure. The thought that the bright heat that flashed between him and Andrea was probably now gone for good was the most chilling thing of all.

He switched on the television, flinging himself down onto the bed and flipping through the channels until he came to one in English. He had no right to push Andrea, trying to make her give more than she was ready to. She'd come to terms with whatever kept her here in her own time. He might be a lost cause, but he couldn't believe the same applied to her.

A knock sounded on the door. When he opened it, she was there, as if all his fantasies had fleshed out and turned into reality. She was holding a printer, a packet of paper balanced precariously on top of it.

'Are you all right?' The question blurted from her lips.

'Yes, I'm fine. You were right, I did need to warm up a bit. Let me take that.' Somehow he managed to relieve her of the printer and paper without touching her.

'Thanks. Look, I'm sorry, Cal. The last few days have been a bit stressful.' She rubbed at her face with her sleeve.

'Forget it. There's nothing to be sorry for. How's Matthew?'

'He's fine. Tomas is looking after him for a minute but I need to get straight back to him.'

Cal imagined that Tomas could manage perfectly well for more than a minute. But he'd already decided not to push Andrea so much. Cal nodded at the printer.

'What's this for?'

'I was wondering if you could print out the photographs you have of Joe. The printer's set up to work on the hotel's Wi-Fi, and I've brought some spare ink cartridges.' She fished in her pocket, bringing out a couple of small boxes.

'No problem. I'll get it done.' That was an unequivocal message. He wouldn't be seeing her again this evening.

Andrea was obviously battling to keep something under wraps, and it was clear he wasn't helping at the moment. Perhaps she'd decided she needed the evening off from him…

'I'll see you tomorrow, then.' Cal turned, dumping the printer onto the bed, and then took the ink cartridges from her hand. This time his fingers brushed her palm. It felt as if a moment's warmth had flashed between them, and then it was gone.

'Yeah. Tomorrow. Um… I should be going. Things to do…' She was edging away from him now.

Suddenly, Cal needed to put things straight between them. He reached forward, taking her by the shoulders, and Andrea stared dumbly up at him.

'Look, Andrea, I know you're under stress at the moment, and I'm sure I haven't made things any better. I'm sorry for that…'

'It's nothing.' Her chin jutted out defensively. 'Everything will be fine for the wedding.'

He wasn't talking about the wedding. He was talking about the one person that he wanted… *needed* to be happy. None of his careful resolve not to get too involved with her would be worth anything if Andrea wasn't happy.

But it all came back to the fact that he felt she needed to talk, and she didn't want to.

What made him think he knew any better than Andrea? It might feel like a lifetime, but he'd only known her a few days.

His hands dropped to his sides, and he nodded. 'I know it will. Forget I said anything.'

The look she gave him set him on fire. Vulnerable, and yet with the strength that came from suffering.

'I appreciate your concern, Cal. But I have to go now.'

'I know. Go.' Cal watched her as she hurried away along the corridor, walking so fast that it looked as if she was going to break into a run any moment.

He went back into his room and closed the door. Leaning back against it, he shut his eyes, murmuring the words he'd really wanted to say to Andrea's face.

Will you please just talk it out with someone, Andrea?

CHAPTER SEVEN

CAL SPENT THE EVENING, and the better part of the following morning hiding out in his room. Just as he was considering ordering brunch, a tap sounded at his door. He'd chased away the friendly cleaning woman who'd knocked earlier, preferring to make his own bed than to risk her vacuuming up the photographs he had laid out on the floor, but he wondered if maybe she was giving him a second try.

'Thanks but...' Cal opened the door, the words drying in his throat. It was Andrea.

She looked bright and just as beautiful as ever in jeans and a patterned sweater. And she was holding a tray.

'I bought you apology hot chocolate.' She nodded down towards two cups, filled to the brim. 'With mortification sprinkles, and embarrassment toasties.'

Suddenly, he was perfectly happy. '*Mortification* sprinkles? How did you know they're my favourite?' Cal stood back from the door. The egg and bacon toasties looked pretty good, as well.

'It was just a wild guess.' She grinned suddenly, stepping into the room. She brought with her the smell of food—making Cal realise just how hungry he was—and a shaft of pure sunshine.

There was nowhere to put the tray since all the available surfaces had been used for the printer and the photographs last night, before Cal had resorted to the floor this morning. Cal took it from her and put it down on the bed, pleased to see that she felt comfortable enough to sit down next to it. He followed suit, taking a seat on the other side of the tray, careful not to tip its contents to one side.

'Look…' They both spoke together, falling silent to let the other one go first. Cal would have listened to anything that Andrea had to say to him, but he needed to say this right now, before she started to apologise again.

'Andrea, you have nothing to apologise for or to feel embarrassed about. This is my fault. I knew that there was something you didn't talk about and I went ahead and pushed you anyway. I'm sorry, and I won't do it again.'

He might have said more. He could have admitted to his reason for pushing her, but Cal wasn't ready to tell her how much she fascinated him, and he doubted there would ever be a time when he would be. But he could make his peace with her. That was important to him beyond the need to work together on the wedding arrangements.

Warmth ignited in her eyes. Cal's one apology was enough to satisfy her, while she just couldn't stop apologising for something that wasn't her fault.

'I shouldn't have—'

'Stop, Andrea. Just stop. You have every right to tell me to back off. Much more explicitly than you did. Let's put an end to this, shall we?'

She nodded, wordlessly. Cal picked up one of the cups from the tray and took a sip from it. 'This is really nice.'

'It's Craig's secret recipe. Our pastry cook. I did a deal with him for it…'

Who wouldn't share their secrets with Andrea? Her practical good sense, her kindness and that edge of fragile vulnerability made it obvious that she'd seen more than she said, and that she could understand anything. She understood Cal well enough already.

'His wife's pregnant. She's Italian and he's from London; he can get by in Italian but he couldn't understand all the leaflets she'd been given. I translated them for him.' Andrea smiled. 'And gave him a bit of advice about not being quite so worried about her.'

'You would have done that anyway, wouldn't you?' Cal took another sip. 'I think you got the better deal.'

'Yes, so do I.'

Cal picked up one of the toasted sandwiches, removing the cocktail stick that bound it all together and taking a bite. He nodded his approval, still chewing, and Andrea finally started to relax, taking a sip of her own drink.

'You've been busy.' She looked at the photographs scattered around the room.

'I printed out everything I thought would do. Seems I have more than I realised.'

'I have too. Perhaps an album isn't really the thing. I could ask the manager if she'll lend me some of the display boards the hotel has for conferences, and use those. She has some full-height ones that are really attractive and they wouldn't be out of place at the reception. Maybe decorate them with some flowers...'

'Sounds great. Much better. What about printing some of the photos a little larger?'

'Yes, that's good.'

He was still curious, but Cal had learned his lesson, and he knew if he pushed Andrea she was going to retreat again. He'd deserve every ounce of silence and every blank look that she could give him. He collected the photographs up from the floor, placing the pile down next to her, so she could look through them while she was eating.

She started to separate them out, picking the best ones to use. When she came to the one that Cal had pondered over the most, she stopped.

'This is…amazing.'

'I'm not sure Maggie will want it in there.' It was one of his favourite photographs of Joe and Maggie but maybe her wedding wasn't the time to remind her of that point in her life.

Andrea thought for a moment, staring at the photograph. 'I think she will. This is what their marriage vows are all about, isn't it? In sickness and in health.'

The photograph showed exactly that. Maggie's face was pale, with dark rings under her eyes, and her head was swathed in a scarf to hide her rapidly thinning hair. But Joe was looking at her as if she was the most beautiful woman in the world. The only one he loved, whatever happened.

'I'll leave that to you. You know her best.' Cal picked up the tray, moving it to a side table, and when he sat back down, Andrea put the photograph onto the 'definite' pile.

'I know she'll want me to include it. She used to tell me that one of the things she loved the most about Joe was that he never stopped looking at her like this, even on her worst days.'

She picked up the next photograph, squinting at it. Then she sighed, her hand dropping to her lap. However much they both tried, it was obvious that hot chocolate and old photographs weren't enough to divert their thoughts.

'Cal, you're right. I want to talk, I just… can't.'

He took a deep breath. Whatever he said next would be crucial.

'Maybe…do things one step at a time. If you don't feel comfortable talking to a friend, then maybe set up an appointment with a professional. A good counsellor will help you get to the point where you feel you can talk in a safe environment.'

She nodded, staring at her fingers, twined impossibly together now. 'Not you?'

'I've lost the right to expect that of you. I gave it away when I pushed you.' Cal felt the corners of his mouth turning down in regret. If he'd only been less sure of himself, and more sure of Andrea.

'You saw…' Suddenly she looked up at him. The distress in her face was enough to make any heart break. 'You saw it, Cal. Maybe the thing I really needed was for someone else to see what I've been trying to ignore.'

He couldn't think of anything to say. He was sure that whatever he *did* say should leave Andrea plenty of space to do whatever she needed to do.

'Will you do something for me? If there's anything you ever need or want... It doesn't matter what it is, just wanting it is enough.'

He expected her to give one of those little nods, that was all they ever needed to signify that they thought the same way on something. But Andrea was studying her hands again.

'You know about Africa, right?'

'I know...that the photographs meant something to you.'

She nodded. 'My dad worked there for a while when I was little. I loved it, and when I graduated from medical school I wanted to go back because it seemed that there was something I could do there. It took a couple of years before I had the right experience...'

This only gave him more questions. But now wasn't the time for Cal to ask; he should be grateful that she was even still speaking to him, let alone saying this much. He should just stay quiet and let her say whatever she wanted to say.

'You know how it is. It can be heartbreaking and challenging, but ultimately you get more out of it than the people you're supposed to be helping.'

'What were you doing out there?'

'You know how it is. Where there's a need, you do whatever has to be done, and I was involved with all kinds of medical care. But my speciality was working with people with disabilities. Helping to provide a framework that would give them opportunities.'

Cal nodded. People like Andrea were much needed everywhere in the world.

'How long were you there?'

'Three years. It was hard, but I loved my work. And I fell in love as well.'

Lucky man. Cal took the thought back immediately, because Andrea had already told him that it had ended badly. Anyone who could love Andrea and make her happy deserved his respect.

'Who…?'

'Judd was a paramedic. He took me under his wing when I first arrived and taught me the ropes. We did a lot of outreach work together, travelling to the more remote places.'

'It's good work.' Cal knew that getting the right people to the right places was half the battle. People living in isolated communities often had to travel many miles to get medical help.

'I thought so. I *think* so…' Andrea hadn't lost the commitment that had made her want to help. She'd lost something else though, and Cal knew that whatever was coming next wouldn't be good.

'We were on our way back from a trip. Judd was driving and we were talking about our leave, back in the UK. All the things we were going to do, the people we'd see. I was so looking forward to introducing him to my parents; Dad would have loved him…' Andrea fell silent for a moment. As if this was a last happy memory and she wanted to keep hold of it for a little while longer.

'The truck hit a pothole. We went off the road, and down a ravine. There had been a lot of rain that spring, and the river had almost burst its banks.'

Andrea was shaking, looking down at her hands, and he reached out, touching her arm just to let her know that he was there. She leaned against him, and he put his arm around her shoulders.

'I don't know how I got Judd out of the truck. I remember the cabin filling with water, and…he was barely conscious. I'd dislocated my shoulder, and it was the most I could do just to get him to the river bank.'

'I wouldn't fancy my chances in those circumstances.' It must have been an almost superhuman effort for Andrea, hampered by a useless arm and blinding pain.

'There was no one to help us. By some miracle my phone worked, and I called our central clinic. But he was too badly injured. He died before they could reach us, and all I could do was hold him.'

'Andrea… I'm so sorry.' There was nothing more he could say. But he could hold her in his arms, and she snuggled against him, seeming to derive some comfort from that.

'Is that why you didn't want me to go down to Matthew, yesterday?' He put his own pride aside, allowing that Andrea might have felt as protective of him as he had of her.

'It was…stupid…'

'It was incredibly brave, Andrea. Most people would have just baulked at it.'

She moved against him, giving a little shrug. But he could tell that his words had pleased her.

'I came home to London, and I was in hospital for a while, and then went to Mum and Dad's in Oxfordshire to recuperate. Maggie was great; I don't think I could have got through it without her.'

'You didn't talk to her about it?'

'I did, and she never minded; she always listened. I suppose I just wanted to get back to something that approached normality and reckoned that I'd said enough. I felt I ought to be moving on.' Andrea gave a little shrug.

'So you made it happen. I can understand that.'

'Yeah. Maggie told me to take things slowly, but I knew better. I'm a doctor, and I should have known how to deal with it but...'

Cal chuckled. 'Doctor heal thyself, you mean? If you've worked out how to do *that*, you'll be the first. We're only human.'

She looked up at him, her face stained with tears. 'Nice to know. I always thought I was indestructible.'

'I reckon I'm indestructible too. But don't tell anyone.' There was more. Maybe Andrea would tell him and maybe not. He would just hold her, and let her make her own decision about that.

'That's the thing, though. I could handle losing Judd. Not easily, but grief's a process and I knew I had to go through it and come out the other side. Somehow, I couldn't bring myself to go back to work, though.'

'From what I've seen of your shoulder, you must have had a fair bit of healing to do there, as well.'

'I did, but that wasn't it. You know how it is when you can't save someone, Cal, but as doctors we have to move on. I couldn't save him. I tried...'

He saw it all, now. The man she loved had died in her arms, and Andrea had been able to do nothing to stop it. It was enough to shatter anyone's confidence.

'You lost your trust in yourself?' He ventured the obvious conclusion.

'Yes. I tried going back to work, but I just froze whenever I had to deal with something on my own. I was more of a liability than anything else. I decided to go away for a while, and found myself here...not here at this hotel, but in a little boarding house in the village. I heard they needed a new doctor, and came up to find out a bit more.'

'And this was something you could deal with?'

A smile spread across her face. 'You're never alone in a hotel, Cal. Twenty-four-hour everything, including medical staff. Tomas and I cover for each other, there's always a nurse on duty, and there are a dozen people who are trained to deal with medical emergencies on the slopes.'

'And you've made sure that everyone rehearses every possible emergency scenario.'

'Yes. The manager wanted someone who'd take the initiative and do that, and I was very motivated in that direction too. I found some peace here. There's something reassuring about waking up and seeing the mountains, still there, every morning.'

'It's a good place, Andrea.' He should never have tried to make Andrea see beyond her life here. Not without knowing what she'd been through.

'It is. But it's not enough for me any more. It hasn't been for some time, but… I don't know how to live and work anywhere else any more.'

Cal hugged her. She clung to him, no longer crying. It was as if their conversation had given her some peace as well, although he had no right to hope that it might.

'You could take your time. Your job doesn't always have to define you.'

Andrea drew back from him, looking him steadily in the eye. Then suddenly she smiled. 'Could you just say that again, please? I want to appreciate just how bizarre it sounds, coming from you.'

Cal chuckled, holding up his hands. 'Yeah.

Okay, I suppose I haven't exactly lived out that principle.'

'Not entirely. Although I can see why it's important to you to hang onto your professional ambitions. You had to battle so hard to do what you wanted to do.'

He flopped onto his back on the bed, covering his eyes with his hands. 'I'm really that transparent?'

'More translucent, I'd say. The lights are obviously on in there, but I'm never quite sure what you'll do next.'

'That's good. I'm not sure what I'll do next, either.'

'Your job? Or the wedding?' She lay down next to him, curling her legs up onto the bed, and propping herself up on her elbow.

'Is this your way of telling me to stop now, because you're done talking? I've learned my lesson, and you can just say it.'

'Stop, then. I'm not really done, I know that, but I'm done for now.'

'And you're okay?' That was the only thing that really mattered to Cal.

'Yes, I'm okay. There's always a light at the end of the tunnel.'

Cal would agree with that, if only he could find where his tunnel was. If he'd been instrumental in helping Andrea find hers, then that was everything he could wish for.

'That sounds like something Maggie would say.'

'She's mentioned it.' Andrea gave a little laugh. 'Once or twice.'

Maggie's matchmaking didn't seem so frivolous now. She was trying to encourage her friend to move on. She might have chosen the wrong man for Andrea to move on with, but Cal could respect the reasoning behind it all.

'So. Cal…'

'Yes?' He had the feeling that something of some import was coming.

'What are you not sure about?'

He'd told no one about this, not even Joe. But Andrea had trusted him…

'It's just my job. I'm not sure whether I should move on or not.'

'You're thinking of leaving your job? I thought you loved it.'

'I do. The board's offered me a new position, as director, and I'm not sure whether to take it or not.'

'Why wouldn't you? Does the promotion mean you'll have less contact with patients?'

'I'd still be operating, and caring for my own patients, but I wouldn't be travelling so much;

I'd need to be in London to keep an eye on things there.'

'And the travel means that much to you?'

Now that she mentioned it, he realised it really didn't, and that he couldn't pin down why he felt so uneasy about taking the job.

'Travel is… really just a way of being somewhere I can make a difference. As the London Director, I'd have the opportunity to make an even greater difference than I do now.'

She pressed her lips together, laying her hand on his chest. Cal wondered if she could feel his heart beat, and whether she knew that right now his heart was beating just for her.

'I guess that for someone who's always prided themselves on making their own decisions, it's difficult to consider something that someone else has suggested.'

Cal turned the idea over in his head. Suddenly his own reticence in taking up what was a once-in-a-lifetime opportunity made a bit of sense.

'Is that a nice way of saying that I'd rather be in control and to have applied for the job myself?'

'If you like. Why don't you imagine that you had, and see how you feel about it then?'

Cal rolled over onto his side, to face her. 'You may have a point. But I don't need to make that decision right now, which means that we can concentrate on photographs for today.'

'Is that your way of telling me that you want to stop now?' She gave him a quizzical look.

'Yeah.' He grinned at her. 'I appreciated the conversation, though.'

'Me too. And now we've got a wedding to arrange.'

CHAPTER EIGHT

THEY'D WAITED UNTIL Maggie and Joe were off skiing for the afternoon and then Cal had helped Andrea carry the boards upstairs. They were a bit more difficult to hide than an album, and, since Maggie was in and out of Andrea's apartment all the time, he'd offered his room.

By the time Andrea had finished her afternoon surgery, Cal had set up the boards. Closeted in his room, sorting through old photographs, was a treat. Andrea had laughed over the photos of Cal and Joe when they were at medical school together, and Cal had insisted that the picture of Maggie and Andrea, aged ten and dressed up for their school's Halloween party, should go into the 'definites' pile.

'No! Not that one!' Andrea snatched the photograph from his hand. 'Goodness only knows what I was thinking.'

'I think you look adorable.' Cal chuckled. 'Sweet sixteen.'

'Even then I should have known better than to wear a neckline like that. I thought it was sophisticated.'

'It's a nice one of Maggie…' Cal gave her a cajoling smile that was immensely difficult to resist.

'There's another one here of her. On her own.' Andrea shuffled through the pile and found it. 'That's much better.'

'Whatever you say. Are you hungry? Since we seem to be on a roll with this, maybe we should get room service?'

Maggie would *love* that if she found out. She would add Cal and Andrea together, multiply them by room service, and total it all up to an I-told-you-so. But Andrea didn't care. It had been a long time since she'd been able to mess around with someone the way she and Cal did. A long time since she'd talked to someone who seemed to understand so completely. Something *had* happened between them. It *was* happening. Just because she had no name for it, didn't mean it wasn't real.

Andrea found the room-service menu hidden under a pile of printer paper. 'What do you fancy?'

He craned his neck to read over her shoulder. Since this morning he'd seemed less reticent in allowing himself to be close to her, and it was an entirely delicious evolution in their relationship.

'Um… I don't know. What's good?'

'I can phone down to the kitchen and get them to send the dish of the day up? That's always nice.'

'Perfect. Half-bottle of wine?'

She probably shouldn't. Andrea needed all the inhibitions she could muster at the moment. But she'd told him her most closely guarded secret already. What did she have left to lose?

'Sounds good. I'll get them to choose something…'

The boards were ready. They were decorated with paper flowers, which matched the colour scheme that Maggie had chosen for the real flowers, and there was a pad of sticky hearts, where the guests could write their own special messages for Maggie and Joe. Andrea and Cal had got together at the end of each day and ticked off the things they'd sorted, reviewing what still needed to be done.

Somehow, and Cal wasn't entirely sure how, they'd made it through the first difficult days here in Italy. The calm after the storm seemed particularly welcome to him, because Andrea seemed happier and more beautiful than ever.

He woke early, on a fine bright day. Stretching lazily in bed reminded him that he'd let his morning exercise regime slip, and he decided that the gym and a few laps in the hotel pool would be in order.

Few people rose at seven o'clock on a Sunday morning when they were on holiday, and he had the gym to himself. Almost… In one corner he could see Andrea, clad in a pair of figure-hugging leggings and a sleeveless vest.

'Morning.' She was concentrating on adjusting one of the machines, and didn't notice his approach.

'Oh, hello. You're up early.' She gave a little frown. 'Not worried about the wedding, are you?'

'No. That all seems to be going quite spectacularly well.'

She laughed. 'Shh. You'll spoil it.'

This suited her. Getting back into a routine and feeling that she was in control of her life. Cal's own routine often amounted to little more than taking each day as it came, assessing which need was the more urgent and hoping that the others would be able to wait.

'I'm over there.' He grinned, pointing to one of the machines in the far corner.

Andrea turned to look. 'Ah, yes. That one's got a rather nice view.'

That wasn't the reason. Working up a sweat

with Andrea seemed like a fine start to the morning, but he didn't want to spoil things. They'd been getting on so well in the last few days.

'I don't suppose you could…' She called after him and Cal turned quickly. Yes. Whatever it was she wanted him to do, the view would be a lot better if Andrea was somewhere in his line of sight.

'I can't get the latch on this machine.'

He walked over and examined the adjustment lever. It wouldn't move and he applied a bit more pressure. 'Looks as if it's stuck. It doesn't want to budge.'

She puffed out an exasperated breath. Obviously she'd been trying to set the machine to offer the least resistance, presumably to accommodate her injured shoulder.

'I'll just have to try something else, then.'

Cal hesitated. It was good to see that Andrea *was* exercising, and maybe he should leave her to it. But in the last few days, she'd stopped trying to hide the effects of her injury, flexing her shoulder whenever it hurt instead of holding her arm stiffly at her side. That alone must have made a big difference.

'You're doing mild resistance exercises?' They were pretty standard for the kind of shoulder injury that Andrea was recovering from. 'Want to try them together?'

'Yes. Thanks.'

Cal swung his leg over the long bench, sitting down. He could gauge the strength of Andrea's shoulder much better than any machine could, and provide exactly the right amount of resistance. She sat down opposite him, astride the bench.

'All right. A little closer. Keep your back straight.'

She moved until her knees were almost touching his. Cal held up his right arm. 'Let's try with your good arm first, so I can see how much strength you have there.'

Andrea grinned. 'You're doing this properly, then.'

There actually wasn't much choice. If she was going to be this close then he needed to have something to concentrate on, other than the blue-grey colour of her eyes. They fascinated him endlessly, changing in response to the light.

'Am I interfering?'

'No, that's okay. I'd like a bit of feedback, I don't get to the physiotherapist as often as I probably should. One of the penalties of being up here.'

She pressed her palm against his, pushing

against it. She was strong, but Cal could see that she wasn't really trying.

'You can do better than that.'

Suddenly the pressure increased. This was turning into a real contest. Cal had positioned his own arm at an awkward angle, so that Andrea's would be in exactly the correct position, and he was beginning to feel the strain.

'Uh. That's enough.' He gave in before she did.

'Sorry... Did I push too hard?' The innocent smile on her lips told Cal that she was enjoying the competitive side of this exercise.

'No. I'm just fine.' Cal rubbed his shoulder, grinning at her. He rather liked this new side to their dynamic, where Andrea was pushing to test her strength against his, rather than pushing him away.

'I wouldn't want to hurt you.'

'You won't. Let's try the other arm, shall we?'

Her other arm was much weaker. Cal could hold his hand in place easily and Andrea was clearly pushing as hard as she could.

'All right. Keep your body straight, the force should be coming from here...' He indicated which muscles she should be using on his own shoulder.

She nodded, trying again. Better posture this time, but less force.

'You haven't been doing these for a while, have you?' He ventured the observation. It was obvious that Andrea had abandoned her exercises for more than just a couple of weeks.

She wrinkled her nose. 'No, I haven't. Would being busy be a good excuse?'

'No, not really.'

'I thought not. I wouldn't take it as one either. How about just not wanting to think about it?'

'Yeah, that'll do.' It was common enough, and in Andrea's situation more than understandable. Her shoulder was strong enough to perform all the everyday tasks she needed to do, probably even for light exercise and sport. But she was continually compensating, and that might well set up long-term problems.

She knew all that. He didn't need to explain, just to stick with her and show her, if he could, that a full recovery was possible. She'd been working at half throttle for a while now and he could see that it was beginning to frustrate her.

'Let's try again. Ten reps will be enough for starters.'

They went through the whole range of exercises and Cal slowly began to push her. Andrea pushed back, harder sometimes than she should, but when he called a halt she stopped. Helping her achieve something had taken over from the physical frisson of contact, and it was a deeper kind of thrill.

'Last one. We need to get this exactly right.' He sat back down on the bench. 'How do you do with backward movement?'

'Not all that well.' She turned the corners of her mouth down. 'That's the most difficult.'

'You want to give it a go?'

Of course she did. *Difficult* was like a red rag to a bull with Andrea. She had the kind of drive that would scatter every obstacle from her path, if only she could bring herself to use it.

She sat astride the bench, pushing herself back until her shoulders almost touched his chest. Cal swallowed hard, trying not to think about it. So far, Andrea's backward movements were just fine...

'Shoulders back.' He rapped out the instruction a little harshly, instinctively obeying it himself. He held out his hands, touching her elbows lightly with his palms.

'Uh. That's no good, is it?' Her right shoulder was noticeably weak and stiff.

'It could be better. You can improve it a lot if you keep working, though.' There was no point in telling her that it wasn't so bad. Andrea knew as well as he did that the shoulder needed some work.

Her body was warm against his. It was hard to remain unresponsive to her scent, and the feel of her so close. Cal closed his eyes and thought of…the wedding.

'Try again. Ten very gentle reps.' Andrea started to push against the pressure of his hand. 'I'm going to have to check out the venues for the stag night. Interested?'

'I can come with you on Tuesday. I'll be going down to the airport to meet some of the wedding guests, and I can put them on the hotel's minibus and meet you in the village afterwards. I'll leave Maggie and Joe to greet them at the hotel.'

'Yeah? Thanks, that would be good.' He could feel the pressure of Andrea's arm begin to falter against his hand. 'That's enough. Rest. You don't want to do too much today; we're skiing tomorrow.'

'Yes, I don't want to miss that. Although I may not be able to keep up with you guys.' It had been decided that tomorrow they'd all take a day off and go skiing together.

'I'm sure you won't have much trouble. Living here gives you much more opportunity to practise.'

'Ah, yes. My wonderful technique makes

up for a lot.' Andrea chuckled. 'I can manage another ten.'

'Okay. Don't push it. Five for starters.'

He was pushing things to the very limit, wanting more of this warmth, more of the relaxed jokes and the underlying competitiveness that added a little spice to it all.

She managed five reps and then stopped. She turned suddenly to give him a smile.

'I think I'm done, now. Thanks, Cal. I don't suppose you could fly in every other morning, for the next six weeks, could you?' Andrea clearly knew that was impossible, but suddenly it didn't seem like such a bad idea.

'You don't need me. You know what to do, it's just a matter of keeping it a part of your routine.' This was what he told all his patients. Their recovery was as much in their hands as it was in his. It was usually an affirmation, a way of giving someone back control of their own body after they'd experienced surgery.

Now it was loss. Not just yet, though…

'What do you say we do this every other morning, until the end of the week? You'll start to see some difference, even after that. And I could do with a few sessions here in the gym.'

'Really?' She unashamedly looked him up and down, and Cal felt a tingle follow the path of her gaze. 'You look like you're in pretty good shape to me.'

He *had* to move now. Cal got up, leaving her sitting on the bench. He was pretty sure that her gaze was still on him, and he resisted the temptation to throw back his shoulders and beat his chest in a primitive response.

'We'll ski tomorrow, and then if your shoulder's okay we'll try a short session on Tuesday morning. I'll come along to the airport if you like and we can go on to the village together.'

Andrea gave that sudden, gleaming smile of hers. 'Are you sure? I imagine you just *love* airports; you must see enough of them.'

'Yeah, I do. They're not so bad. The airport's always the start of something new.'

'Ah, well, in that case you can definitely come. First round's on me when we get to the village.'

'You're on. What are you doing today?'

'Consulting my list. Checking it twice...'

Cal chuckled. 'I'll catch up with you, then, when I've finished here. We can check both our lists together.'

CHAPTER NINE

IT WAS NICE having Cal around. He'd helped her take those first tentative steps yesterday morning, which marked her commitment to making a full recovery from her operation, instead of one that was just good enough. Afterwards, he hadn't minded wrapping little treats and gifts for the wedding while Andrea caught up with her emails.

The more normal routine of bumps, bruises, strains and the odd cut had reasserted itself in the medical suite. Tomas was managing perfectly well without her so Andrea could get on with her preparations for the wedding.

Monday dawned bright and clear, a perfect day for skiing. Andrea sat at her dressing table, carefully smoothing oil onto her scars.

She hadn't done that in a while, either. Sometimes the operation scar pulled a little and she'd started to just ignore it, along with the other jagged scar from the accident. But now she felt a little more conscious of them both. She just hadn't looked before, hadn't considered the possibility that the appearance of her scars could be improved. Why bother, when everything else was in ruins around her? Now, the possibility of something more shone brightly in the distance. A long way away, still, but it was there.

'We're not going to mention the W-E-D-D-I-N-G, today,' Maggie announced when the four of them were assembled in the reception area at the hotel. 'We're taking a break.'

Joe pulled a face of mock despair. 'You want a break already? We're not even married yet.'

'Not from you.' Maggie planted a kiss on his cheek. 'From everything else. Andrea and I have been working really hard to get everything organised. There's so much to think about.'

'Fair enough. I'm sure we've been doing a lot too, eh, Cal?'

Cal scratched his nose, grinning. 'Choosing the waistcoats was a tough one.'

'Yeah. Yeah, that was particularly gruelling.'

They might joke about it, but Cal had been there for her, just as much as Joe had been there for Maggie. And maybe it would be good to take a break from talking about the wedding, just for today.

They'd decided on a one-day ski tour, which would take them on an easy route up into the mountains, and then back down again at sunset. The group of ten was led by Francine and Bruno, who set off at the head of the party.

Out here in the mountains was the perfect place to forget about everything. The pace was brisk enough to keep everyone occupied, but there was time to stop and catch their breath, and to appreciate the snowscape around them.

'How are you doing?' Cal too seemed to have left his worries back at the hotel. A warm beanie and wraparound reflective sunglasses, along with the fact that he hadn't shaved this morning, gave him a relaxed air.

'Fine.' Andrea knew the real intent of his question. 'My shoulder didn't hurt this morning, but I've put a support on, just as a precaution.'

They trekked together silently, up a long, steep slope. At the top, Francine called a halt for everyone to rest and admire the view.

'It's difficult, isn't it? Now that Maggie's put an embargo on mentioning the you-know-what, it's all I can think about.'

'What, out here? Cal, look around you.'

'Yeah, I know.' He laughed, propping his sunglasses on the rim of his hat. 'It's beautiful.'

He swung round, his gaze finding hers, just

for a moment, but there was no question about his intended meaning. She was beautiful, too. Even after all she'd shown him of the uglier side of her life, he thought her beautiful.

'Cal, I've been thinking…and I want to apologise.'

'Again? What have you done this time?'

'I didn't make things very easy for you when you arrived. You were only trying to help.'

He grinned. 'I like a challenge.'

'Don't, Cal… I know I behaved badly.' The thought had been preying on Andrea's mind for days.

'You were protecting yourself. And I didn't respect that.' He turned the corners of his mouth down. 'You really don't have anything to apologise for.'

'Perhaps I should think a bit more carefully about who I choose to protect myself from.' The look in his eyes told Andrea that she'd been right in feeling that this was a sore spot for Cal. He really didn't like the thought that Andrea had been protecting herself from him, and when she thought about it, Andrea didn't much like it either.

'I'll leave you to make those decisions. And in the meantime, I'm going to take a leaf out of Maggie's book and ban a word. Today isn't a day to be S-O-R-R-Y about anything.'

It wasn't. Cal stayed by her side as they trekked further into the mountains, making tracks in the fresh snow. It was enough that he was there. Everything was all right between them, and the silence warmed her.

Bruno had gone on ahead, and by the time they reached the log cabin he'd lit the wood-burning stove. Thick soup was bubbling in a pan, and the cabin was warming up.

Joe and Cal were arguing amicably about something and Maggie slipped her arm around Andrea's. 'I can see why you love it here. It's so…fresh. Clean. It's a good place for new starts.'

Maggie had made a new start. She was putting the cancer behind her, along with all the pain and worry it had brought. She and Joe were solid, and all they'd been through together had only brought them closer.

'It's a great place for new starts. Perfect for a…' Andrea stopped herself before she said it. 'A *you-know-what*.'

Maggie chuckled. 'Glad you're keeping to the rules. Yes, I'm glad we decided on here. Not least because you're here and we can spend some time together. I miss you.'

'I'll be back. I'm not sure when…'

'I know. That's okay. In the meantime, I can

still miss you, can't I?' Maggie grinned at her friend.

It was on the tip of Andrea's tongue, but she didn't say it. She was beginning to think she might leave here sooner than Maggie thought, but she wasn't quite ready to make any firm decisions yet. It was as Cal had said. Building new muscle took time, and that applied to emotional muscle as well.

'Yes, you can miss me. I miss you too.'

They spent an hour at the cabin, leaving it spick and span for the next group who would be arriving. Francine pulled a large block of chocolate from her pack, leaving it by the stove to replace the one that had been opened and shared around amongst the party.

It was all perfectly timed. The sun was going down as they reached a high ridge above the hotel and they stopped to take it all in. Golden light bathed the mountain tops, as the valleys became dark with shadow. Maggie flung her arms around Joe's neck, kissing him.

'There's one for the board.' Cal had taken his camera from the pouch inside his jacket and he showed Andrea the small display screen at the back. He'd caught their friends in an embrace, silhouetted against the sunset.

'That's gorgeous. Does that mean we can

take down the one of Maggie and me having a water fight, and replace it with this?' Two little girls, both soaked to the skin and still trying to get each other even wetter than they already were.

'No. I particularly like that one; something else is going to have to go.' Cal put his camera back into the pouch. He didn't take many photographs, nor did he walk around with his camera in his hand all the time. But from time to time, he'd see something that he knew would make a good photograph and take the shot.

'You're not going to take any more?'

Cal shook his head. 'That was the one I wanted. I'd prefer to just enjoy this first hand.'

He put his arm around her shoulders. The way a good friend might do. Cal wasn't a good friend or a lover—they hadn't known each other long enough for either—but it felt right somehow. As if that was where she belonged.

'Maggie's watching…'

He chuckled. 'Fair enough. Is she taking photographs?'

'No. She isn't as bold as we are.'

He was very close. Andrea could almost feel Maggie's gaze boring into the back of her head, but her friend was too far away to see exactly what was happening between her and

Cal. And Joe would surely keep her from borrowing Francine's binoculars…

Somehow it didn't seem right. Cal's kisses were wonderful, but it was the bond of honesty that had been formed between them that made them so special. And kissing out here, in front of everyone, wouldn't be honest because they'd both decided that they couldn't contemplate a relationship.

His gaze held hers for several heartbeats. The span of a kiss, and then another. Then they turned together towards the sunset.

As the sun disappeared behind the mountains, a spark in the half-light drew Cal's attention. 'What's Bruno doing?'

'Wait and see. They always do this…' One of the other instructors from the hotel had come up to meet them, carrying four long torches, which Bruno had staked into the snow. When he lit them, flames jumped high into the air.

Francine took two of them, and Bruno the other two. They looked at each other nodding a countdown, and at the same moment they both launched themselves onto the slope.

It was a complex fire dance that never failed to thrill Andrea. The instructors all prided themselves on it and practised regularly, but all the artifice of balance and co-ordination was subsumed in the magic of trails of fire that wound their way down in the darkness. She took Cal's arm and snuggled against him. He was the only person she wanted to share this with.

Francine and Bruno reached the bottom and everyone cheered and applauded. The third instructor was giving out electric torches so the trekkers could hold them up as they descended, and at the bottom of the slope Bruno threw one of his flaming torches theatrically in the air, spinning it like a Catherine wheel.

'Andrea… Andrea!' Maggie and Joe were making their way towards her, Maggie waving excitedly.

'Wasn't that wonderful? Do you think… I don't want to impose but…might they do that for the wedding?'

'Don't mention the wedding!' Both she and Cal chorused the words, and Joe laughed.

'But this is different! Would it be out of order if you just asked…?'

'I promise I'll ask them, but I can't promise a yes.'

Andrea saw Cal's lips twitch before he straightened his face. He'd read the wedding folder, including the part she hadn't shown Maggie. When Andrea had mentioned the possibility to Francine, she'd told her that the instructors would have been insulted *not* to be asked. Eight of them were already practising a new descent formation, which would take place at sunset when Maggie and Joe were cutting the cake, and Francine had promised Andrea that it would be spectacular.

'Thank you.' Maggie seemed content with Andrea's diffident reply. 'I'm sure they might be busy or something. It's terribly short notice but it would be lovely.'

Cal stepped in, relieving Andrea of the temptation to tell her friend everything. He took Maggie's arm, and began to walk towards the instructor who was giving out the torches. 'If they can't do it, I'll do it myself for you, Maggie. Naked. With a rose between my teeth.'

The joke had the desired effect. Maggie screamed with laughter, digging her elbow into Cal's ribs, and Joe made a comment about wanting to see that.

'So I'll cancel with Francine, then.' She murmured the words as they joined the line of skiers making their way downhill. 'What colour rose would you like me to get you?'

Cal chuckled. 'Better get blue. It'll match my fingers.'

Their second morning in the gym together left Cal quietly satisfied. It was too soon for Maggie's shoulder to show any improvement, but she was more focussed. He had always felt that the continuation of therapeutic exercise was a matter of self-care and getting into the right head space, and Andrea was more careful about getting her posture exactly right today.

The hotel's minibus was waiting for them in the village for the journey to the airport to pick up the wedding guests who were arriving on the noon flight. As they waited at the gates, Andrea was getting more and more excited.

'How long is it since you've seen your parents?'

'Three months. I stayed with them for a couple of weeks before the season got started, and we video conference once a week, but it's not the same.'

The passengers began to file through the gates, and Andrea waved whenever she recognised someone. Cal accompanied the first arrivals over to the luggage carousel, helping them lift their suitcases off, while Andrea greeted the next group and pointed them in his direction.

Then he heard her calling out. A couple in their fifties were walking towards her, smiling.

'Mum! Dad!' Andrea hugged her mother and then her father. Turning, she beckoned Cal over.

'This is Cal, Joe's best man. Cal, this is my mum, Linda, and my dad, George.'

Cal shook Linda's hand, feeling it cool in his. She was a slight woman and seemed tired from the trip, her dark eyes a little faraway in their gaze. George's grip was firm and assured and his smile was broader. He had white curls and blue-grey eyes that were a lot like Andrea's.

'Cal. Andrea's told me that you're a doctor, as well.'

'Yes.' The thought that some of Andrea's precious video-conferencing time had been spent talking about him was gratifying. 'You've worked in Africa, I hear.'

'That was a long time ago. I'd like to sit down with you, though, and hear about your travels. Andrea says that you're involved with setting up medical facilities all over the world. I'd be interested to hear what's changed since I worked abroad. Lin—?' George broke off suddenly, looking round at his wife.

Linda swayed slightly, and then her legs seemed to just crumple under her. Cal had to move fast to catch her before she hit the floor. She was dead weight in his arms, and he picked her up, carrying her over to a line of seats.

George was at his side, helping him to lay

Linda down and rolling up his jacket to put under her head. But when Cal looked quickly over his shoulder, Andrea was standing stock-still.

All the colour had drained out of her face, and she was trembling, seeming not to notice the people hurrying back and forth around her.

'George...' He heard Linda's voice and focussed his attention back on her, silently willing Andrea to come to her senses. He knew why this must be such a shock to her, but she'd come so far in the past week. If she froze now, it would be yet another knock to her confidence.

There was nothing he could do about that now. George was kneeling beside his wife and he shouldn't be left to deal with her alone.

'Just lie still for a minute, Lin.'

'I'm all right.' Linda tried to sit up, and George gently stopped her. 'I think I must have fainted...'

George smiled at his wife, the same warmth registering in his eyes that Cal had seen in Andrea's. 'Stay there for a minute, love. I just want to make sure you're all right.'

'But, George—'

'Do as Dad says, Mum.' Andrea's voice sounded clear and firm behind him. Cal got out of the way, allowing her to bend down beside her mother.

Andrea reached forward, placing her hand on her mother's forehead. 'You've not got a fever. Any headaches?'

George got to his feet, standing next to Cal, his gaze flipping from his wife to his daughter. 'We'll let Andrea see to her mother.'

Cal nodded. Both men were of the same mind, that Andrea needed to be the one to do this. She was asking all the right questions, doing all the right things. Cal wondered if George was ticking off each possibility in his mind, the same way he was.

Finally, Andrea helped her mother to sit up, turning to face them. 'She's all right. She just fainted.'

'I told you so, dear.' Some colour was beginning to return to Linda's cheeks. 'We should have had breakfast before we came out.'

The other wedding guests were standing in a small knot beside the luggage carousel. An elderly woman in a bright purple windcheater stepped forward, jabbing her finger at his arm. Cal had been told that this was Aunt Mae, but, since everyone seemed to call her that, it wasn't entirely clear whose aunt she was.

'Is she all right?'

'She fainted, Aunt Mae. Have you got any water in your handbag, please?' Andrea answered for him.

The question seemed an odd one, but Aunt Mae began to rummage in her flight bag, producing a bottle of water and a plastic cup. Andrea collected them, sitting back down beside her mother and pouring the water for her.

'I've got a sandwich as well.'

'No, thanks, Aunt Mae, I'm feeling better now.' Linda smiled at her. 'Thanks for the water.'

'You should have something to eat.' Aunt Mae wasn't going to take no for an answer. 'Ham and tomato.'

Linda gave in to the inevitable. 'Maybe just a bite, then. If you could break a little piece off...'

'That's all right.' Mae produced a film-wrapped sandwich from her bag, handing it to Andrea. 'I've got another one. Eating something will make you feel better.'

Andrea accepted the sandwich, moving her father's jacket so that Aunt Mae could come and sit down next to Linda. As George shrugged the coat back on, he turned to Cal.

'Three doctors in attendance, and it turns out that Aunt Mae's got the remedy in her handbag. Typical, eh?'

Cal laughed, nodding in agreement. He was so proud of Andrea. Anyone would have forgiven her for panicking when she saw her mother taken ill so unexpectedly. She'd needed a moment, but she'd pulled herself together and come to help. He could see the pride in George's eyes too as he looked at his daughter.

He wished he could stay but the other guests were still standing by the carousel, not sure what to do next. He walked over to them, assuring everyone that Linda was quite all right, and shepherding them out of the airport and into the waiting minibus.

When he returned, George was retrieving his and Linda's suitcases from the luggage carousel. Andrea walked to the minibus with her mother, helping her in, while Cal and the driver finished loading up the boot.

As he got into the bus, Andrea caught his arm. 'I'm sorry, Cal. I don't think I can make tonight…'

'That's okay. I'm going to come back to the hotel as well.' He wanted to be there for Andrea, if she needed to talk.

'Thanks.' She shot him a glistening smile and Cal went to sit down next to Aunt Mae, who was busy handing round a packet of extra-strong peppermints.

Cal was right where she'd expected him to be, sitting in one of the armchairs in the reception area with a cup of hot chocolate and an English newspaper. He liked busy places, and seemed to be able to concentrate even though people were moving back and forth all around him. Andrea sat down in the chair opposite his.

'Hey. How's your mum?' He looked up from the paper, putting it aside.

'She's fine. Dad and I have been through the entire medical dictionary together, and our joint medical opinion is that she fainted.'

Cal chuckled. 'Must be challenging having a husband and a daughter who are doctors.'

'Must be. My brother's a doctor as well.'

He winced. 'No wonder she prefers to listen to Aunt Mae. Whose aunt is she, by the way?'

'No one's, actually. She's Maggie's mother's next-door neighbour, and Maggie and I have known her since we were kids. She used to ask us to tea and we'd have soda water in china cups and little cakes. We thought we were very grown up.'

'And she always has a sandwich in her handbag?'

'Always. She takes a bottle of water and a sandwich with her when she goes shopping, and sits down and has them in the library. You're not supposed to eat in there, but they all know her and turn a blind eye.'

'She's great. She was telling me all about ancient Sami warriors from northern Finland on the minibus. Apparently the women used to fight with bows and arrows on skis.'

'She's a mine of information; her house is full of books. When I went to medical school, she gave me a twenty-pound note in an envelope, and told me to spend it on going out and having fun. She said I was going to be a fine doctor, like my dad…' Andrea felt her lip quiver. Aunt Mae had made a big mistake on that score.

'You *are* a fine doctor.' Cal was looking at her steadily.

'I froze, Cal.' He'd seen her do it and it was impossible for him to deny it.

'I know. And then you pulled yourself together and made sure that she was all right.'

'It wasn't too difficult. Even Aunt Mae knew that she'd only fainted.' Andrea heaved a sigh. It was okay. She knew her limitations. She'd just dared to think that one day she might break through those barriers.

'Andrea, there's a reason why I wouldn't operate on a member of my family. It's because I'm too personally involved with them. Are you telling me you should feel nothing when your own mother collapses?'

Andrea shrugged. 'No, I suppose not.'

'You had every reason to freeze after what you've been through. What matters is that you helped her. She could have been really ill and you had no way of knowing that. But I saw you check her over and you did it thoroughly without worrying her. You are a *very* fine doctor.'

Andrea's head was reeling. Cal was asking her to believe in herself. And somehow that suddenly wasn't so hard, because *he* believed in her.

'In that case…thank you.'

He gave her a quizzical look. 'Is that all you have to say?'

'Yes. I think it is. Thank you, Cal.'

He smiled. 'Seems I'm more persuasive than I thought.'

'Seems you are.' Andrea looked at her watch. 'Do you still want to go down to the village? We've got enough time to look at the places on my list if we're quick.'

He shook his head. 'No. I think I'd rather stay here and have an early night.'

That sounded as if it was for her benefit. Andrea felt as if she could do with an early night, and probably looked that way too.

'But we won't have another chance. Maggie and Joe's parents are flying in tomorrow morning, and then there's the rehearsal in the afternoon, and we'll all be having dinner together afterwards. Then on Thursday it's the stag and hen nights.'

'You choose a place. You've already made the list, you may as well. Where would you go?'

'But it's a stag night. I've never been on one of those before.'

He rolled his eyes. 'Andrea, if I was taken ill, there's no one I'd rather have around than you. If I can trust you with that, then I'm sure I can trust you to choose a good place for Joe's stag night.'

There was a note of exasperation in his tone. And Cal always told the truth, particularly when he was exasperated. The thought that he really did trust her lifted some of the weight that had been pressing on Andrea's chest for the last couple of hours.

'Okay. There's a little family-run place about five minutes' walk from the funicular railway. They do great food, good beer, and it's a really relaxed atmosphere. Later on in the evening there's music and lots of singing. How does that sound?'

He gave her a delicious smile. 'It sounds perfect. Sorted.'

CHAPTER TEN

EVERYONE HAD ARRIVED SAFELY, the rehearsal
had been relaxed, and now the stag night had
gone smoothly. Cal had counted everyone onto
the funicular railway and then back off again.
He and Joe had agreed that it was one of the
better stag parties they'd attended, before Joe
went to find Maggie. Cal should go and get a
good night's sleep now, but there was one thing
he had to do before he turned in.

As he said his farewells to everyone, shaking
their hands and wishing them a good night, he
saw Joe walk back towards the lift with Maggie. They were laughing together, Joe's arm
around Maggie's shoulders. Maggie's choice of
wardrobe—a pair of sheepskin boots teamed
up with a towelling robe—was a bit of a give-
away for where he might find Andrea.

He walked through the bar and out onto
the wide veranda. At the far end, the hot tub
was surrounded by light and shadow, and as

he approached it he could see a figure resting against one corner of the large hexagonal tub, luxuriating in the bubbles.

'Hey there.' Andrea saw him coming and gave him a wave. 'How did it go?'

'Good. The bar was great, and everyone's in one piece. Yours?'

'We had a lovely time. Maggie's just left with Joe.' Andrea half swam towards him, holding her cocktail glass up above the bubbles, but it slipped out of her hand. 'Oops.'

Cal squatted on his heels, chuckling. Andrea was watching the glass bob up and down on the surface of the water, and he pulled up his sleeve, retrieving it.

'So how drunk are you?'

She raised her eyebrows. 'Not even slightly. I've been on virgin cocktails all night. I wanted to make sure everything went well.'

'Me too. Only it was non-alcoholic beer.'

She quirked her mouth down. 'Too bad. So you're not even a little bit tipsy?'

Andrea gave all the appearance of being a little tipsy herself. Maybe it was the stars above their heads, relief that the evening had gone well, or maybe just relaxing with her friends had that heady, bright-eyed effect on her.

'Now that it's all over, and we don't have

to worry about anyone else, would you like a drink?'

'Only if you join me. It's wonderful in here.'

Too much temptation. Far too much. And Cal was only human...

He hurried up to his room, changing into his bathing trunks. He wrapped one of the warm towelling bathrobes that the hotel supplied around him, and made a detour to the bar on the way back.

'Ooh! Champagne.' She grinned at him as he traversed the heated tiles that led to the tub. Cal propped the bottle in the snow, shivering in the night air as he hurriedly took off his robe and got into the tub.

'Ahh. This is very relaxing.' The warm bubbles against his skin almost took him by surprise. His eyes were telling him that they were surrounded by snow, but the rest of his senses were registering a delicious heat. Made no less delicious by the fact that he was sharing a tub with Andrea.

'Isn't it? I could almost *be* drunk.'

But she wasn't. Andrea was just relaxed and happy, and seeing her like this made Cal's own head swim a little.

He reached out of the tub, pouring two

glasses of champagne and handing one to her. 'What shall we drink to?'

'A successful night. Joe and Maggie tucked up safe and sound together.'

'Sounds good to me. Joe and Maggie.'

He tipped his glass against hers. He was caught in her gaze, and the first sip of champagne seemed to go right to his head. He drifted over to the other side of the tub, in an effort to gather his senses, but Andrea was entrancing, tonight.

It wasn't just the stars above their heads or the champagne. Her curls were caught up at the back of her head, and her neck formed a perfect curve that he could contemplate all night. Her cheeks were pink, and beneath the bubbles he could catch a tantalising glimpse of slim legs.

'So. Give me all the gossip, then. Did Joe's uncle Pete have one too many?'

'He was heading that way. I ordered him a few rounds of non-alcoholic beer, and he never knew the difference.'

'Good thinking. Maggie was a little worried he might get out of order and spoil the evening.'

'He was fine. Going somewhere where we could have something to eat made a big difference. Joe's little brother took a shine to one of the girls on the next table to us, and spent most of the evening chatting to her.'

'Fabulous. Did he get her number?'

'After a fashion. He wrote it on his hand, but it's probably worn off by now. She said she wanted to give him a call so I texted her his number.'

'Nice. You're *really* good at this. What about Joe's grandfather? Did he stay the course?'

'You're joking, right? Grandpa Dave had more stamina than all of us. He wanted to go on somewhere else but I managed to persuade him to get the last train back with us. He told me that young people these days don't know how to have a good time.'

'Mm. He might be right. Maggie's grandmother wanted to know when the male strippers were going to turn up, and she was very disappointed when I told her that Maggie would have been completely mortified at the thought, and I hadn't booked any.' Andrea grinned at him. 'So were you a bit rowdy?'

'It was a stag night. Of course we were rowdy.'

Andrea nodded in approval. 'Yes, so were we. I feel so much better about the wedding now. I really needed a good night out.'

She held her glass out and Cal took it, refilling it along with his. It had been a good evening but *this* was the best part. It felt like coming home and finding Andrea there waiting for him—having a drink together, taking the time to relax and talk about the day.

And then what? Just appreciating the silence as they were now? Warm in the knowledge that the person he was with was his soulmate, and that they could face whatever the morning threw at them together?

Maybe reaching for her in the night. Cal adjusted the emphasis. *Definitely* reaching for her in the night. Knowing that she would want him as much as he wanted her.

Falling in love with her seemed only a whisper away tonight, but it still wasn't enough. Cal had struggled so hard to walk his own path in life that he couldn't imagine sharing it with someone else. Joe and Maggie seemed to do it effortlessly, merging their hopes and dreams into one. But Cal wasn't sure that he'd ever have whatever it was that allowed them to do that.

'It's getting late.' Something in Andrea's eyes told him that she didn't want the evening to end, either.

'Yeah. I guess we should both go and get

some sleep. Busy day tomorrow.' His regret must have shown in his face, because she smiled and gave a little nod.

Cal got out of the pool, feeling the tang of cold air on his skin. Wrapping himself quickly in his robe, he picked Andrea's up and held it open for her. She climbed out of the tub, slipping her arms into the sleeves and knotting the robe tightly around her waist.

'Thank you.' She smiled up at him. 'Best part of my evening.'

'Mine too.' He picked up the bottle of champagne. 'You want to take this with you?'

She thought about it and then shook her head. 'Thanks, but no. There's a little too much there for me, and I wouldn't want to waste it.'

Nothing was wasted on Andrea. If she'd taken just one sip then the whole bottle would have been worth it.

'Put it in the fridge, with a spoon in the top. That's supposed to keep it fresh, isn't it?'

'Mmm. Never sure if that really works or not. They've got some champagne stoppers behind the bar for just this situation. Let's go and see whether *they* work.'

Cal was beginning to feel the cool of the air on his skin now, and he hurried her inside. His last vision of Andrea was of seeing her walk away from him, swathed in a white towelling robe, a half-bottle of champagne dangling from her hand.

And it took all his strength of will not to follow her.

Andrea woke with one thought crisp and clear in her mind.

Cal.

He was just as beautiful as she'd imagined he would be. Strong shoulders, and the kind of chest that was just made to run your fingers across. The steam rising from the water had liquefied on his skin and in his hair, making him look even more delicious. And the best thing about him was that Andrea was sure that Cal knew exactly how to use those slim hips and sensitive fingers, that he was a man who would make love with his head and his heart, and that both of those could be tender and commanding in exactly the right measure.

Maggie had been right. Cal *was* a great guy, and he *was* just what she needed. Andrea sat bolt upright in bed. Maggie. Joe. The Wedding! How could she have forgotten?

Cal, that was how. He could drive every other thought from her head with just a smile. Last night had been perfect and the best part of it had been him.

But now she had things to do. Lots of them. Andrea got out of bed, heading purposefully for the shower.

'Cal, I don't suppose you could help Maggie's grandmother, could you? She's lost one of her hearing aids…' Andrea's morning had been spent facing a thousand last-minute catastrophes, and she'd somehow managed to find a solution for all of them. Now she was busy with the flowers for the room where the reception would be held.

'Yeah, sure. Where is she?'

'Um…not quite sure. Looking for her hearing aid, I think…' Andrea looked around for the florist but she seemed to have disappeared as well.

'Okay. If she's found the hearing aid, does that mean she's lost now?'

Suddenly today didn't seem quite so much of an uphill battle. Cal's dry humour always made things less daunting.

'Yes, I suppose it does.'

'Okay, just so I know. I'll make sure that Maggie's grandmother is in the same place as both of her hearing aids, and that we know where that is.'

Andrea laughed, feeling the tension in her chest ease. 'That would be great. Thanks.'

Her phone buzzed and she took it out of her pocket. 'Oh, no! Why didn't Craig call Tomas? He's on duty today.'

'What's the matter?'

'One of the cooks has fallen down the stairs. They don't think he's hurt but they want me to go down there.'

'I can do that if you like.'

'Would you? I know it's a bit much to ask, but I really need to find the florist.'

'You get on. Consider the cook and Maggie's grandmother sorted.'

He made everything so much easier. Andrea leaned towards him, kissing him on the cheek. 'Thank you so much, Cal.'

She felt the light brush of his fingers on her waist before she stepped back again. How so little could make her feel so much was a mystery—one of those fabulous, enchanting mysteries that could keep you guessing for hours. Now that she'd seen him without most of his clothes, his touch was even more potent.

'My pleasure.' He made that sound as if it referred to the kiss.

'Oh, you know how to get downstairs to the kitchen? Go into the restaurant and tell them you're the doctor, and you need to see Craig.'

'Gotcha.' He turned, and Andrea watched as he walked away.

One more moment of calm, still pleasure. Then Andrea turned her attention back to the flowers.

The strap had been glued back onto the youngest bridesmaid's sandal. Maggie's grandmother had thanked her for sending that nice young man to help her with her hearing aids. Cal had texted to say that the cook was all right, and Andrea had shown Joe's little brother how to knot a bow tie.

Maggie had seemed to float through it all. Her dress was fine, she could find the diamond earrings that her parents had given her, and she hadn't fallen prey to a plague of spots. Andrea had taken the half-bottle of champagne, along with two glasses, to Maggie's room.

'Ooh, champagne!' Maggie took a sip. 'It's the good stuff as well. Where did you get that from?'

'It was left over from last night.' Maggie would have been delighted to hear that she and Cal had been sharing it, but that was something that Andrea wanted to keep for herself. She tipped her glass against Maggie's.

'I'd like to propose a toast. Maggie, you're the most beautiful, lowest-maintenance bride I've ever seen. It's a real honour to be your bridesmaid.'

Maggie flung her arms around Andrea, almost spilling champagne down the back of her neck. 'You've done so much for me, Andrea. Where would I be without you?'

Andrea laughed. 'Maybe the same place I'd be without you. I suppose at least we'd be together.'

'Mmm. Together always. That's nice.' Maggie took another swallow of champagne. 'Now, why don't you sit down for a moment? I'll go and fetch your dress for tonight's dinner, and press it for you.'

'No! You're not supposed to be doing that.'

'Don't be silly. You've been running around after everyone else, can't I do something for you?'

'The only thing that you can do for me is to enjoy your wedding day. Anyway, I wouldn't mind half an hour to myself, just to get ready.'

Maggie nodded. 'Okay. I'll see you downstairs, then.'

It took Andrea three quarters of an hour to get ready, most of which was spent luxuriating in a hot shower. It had been a busy day, but everything was done now. The wedding would go off without a hitch tomorrow.

By the time she arrived in the main restaurant, everyone was seated and the waiters were dispensing drinks. She looked around for Cal, but couldn't see him. How could a room full of friends and family seem empty without him?

As she opened her bag to take out her phone, she felt it vibrate. He must be on his way... Andrea opened his text.

Wedding emergency!

Andrea frowned. There was just enough information to send a tingle of alarm down her spine and not enough to reassure.

But it's okay. We can fix things.

Right. Now she was really worried. Her phone buzzed again as the next instalment of his text arrived.

Don't tell Maggie or Joe.

Maggie and Joe were sitting together and someone had proposed a toast. The clinking of glasses and a round of applause drowned out Andrea's exasperated words.

'You didn't need to tell me that, Cal.'

She started to type a return text but her phone buzzed again.

Get away when you can and meet me in the kitchen. Everything's going to be fine.

Going over to the table and sitting down until she could think of a reason to tear herself away wasn't going to work. Andrea walked over to Maggie, who turned and pulled the empty seat next to her back from the table.

'At last! Where were you?' Maggie's face was shining.

'I had a long, hot shower. And… I'm sorry, I've been called away. Nothing major, I won't be more than a few minutes…'

'That's okay. A doctor's work is never done, eh?'

'Um…no.' Maggie had provided her with as good an excuse as any. 'I'll be as quick as I can.'

'We'll save some champagne for you.' Joe leaned over, smiling.

'Great, thanks. I'll be back in two ticks.'

Andrea hurried down to the kitchen. They were busy with the meal for tonight, and she couldn't see Cal amongst the to and fro. But he'd obviously been watching for her, and after a few moments she saw him striding towards her.

'I didn't mean for you to come straight away…'

'Cal, what is there about "wedding emergency" that doesn't imply urgency?'

He frowned. 'Yes, I suppose that was a little over the top. I just meant for you to come as soon as you could.'

It wasn't like Cal to panic over anything. 'Cal, you're really worrying me now. Just get it over with and tell me what's wrong.'

He wordlessly took her hand, leading her over to the large larder at the far end of the kitchen. Craig, the pastry chef, was hovering by the door, and Cal led the way inside.

'We can fix this. I have a plan...' He seemed intent on giving her the good news first, when Andrea was only really interested in the bad news. She could deal with that, whatever it was.

Or...maybe not.

'Cal! What happened?' Maggie's beautiful wedding cake was lying on the long bench that ran along one wall. In about a million pieces.

'The guy who fell down the stairs...he was carrying the wedding cake.'

'What? What was he doing carrying the wedding cake around? He's all right though, isn't he?'

'Yes, he's fine. He might have a couple of bruises. Craig told him to take it upstairs so they could check what it looked like in situ.'

Andrea rolled her eyes. 'Couldn't they just have imagined what it would look like?'

Cal shrugged. 'We can't blame the kitchen staff. We did make a bit of a thing about checking that everything was going to be perfect.'

'Oh, so it's *my* fault, is it?' After she had navigated so many small problems today, this unexpected disaster was threatening to overwhelm Andrea.

'No, I didn't mean it like that. It's no one's fault, it was an accident, and, to be honest, I'd rather see the cake in pieces than the cook.'

'You're right. Of course you are.' Andrea pressed her hand against her chest in an attempt to slow her racing heart. 'I'm going to take a breath…'

'That sounds like a good idea. I think I'll join you.' Cal made a visible effort to steady himself. 'Why are we panicking so much? If my hand shook like this in the operating theatre, I'd be out of a job.'

'You know what to do in the operating theatre. How many culinary disasters have you dealt with lately?'

'You've got a point. Perhaps we should pretend we're doing an emergency appendectomy…'

'Whatever works, Cal. What are we going to do?'

'I have a plan. I told Craig that we'd need a new cake, three actually, as there are three tiers, and they're already in the oven. He's done three different kinds: carrot cake for the bottom layer, then chocolate, then red velvet for the top tier.'

'Oh. That sounds rather nice. Red velvet, you say?'

'Yeah. Don't imagine that just because I'm passing on the message it means I know what a red velvet cake is.'

'It's a bit like devil's food cake, only it has cocoa instead of chocolate.'

Cal grinned. 'There. I thought you'd know more about cake than I do. Anyway, Craig says they'll be fine for tomorrow. He's going to put them in the large chiller cabinet to cool, and make a white buttercream icing…'

Andrea nodded. 'That's right. We won't have time for marzipan and royal icing.'

'Yes he mentioned that, too. It'll all be ready by tomorrow.'

'Are you sure?' Cal's optimism was heartening, but Andrea wasn't sure whether it was based on hard facts. 'It'll take most of the night to decorate it, and we can't ask Craig to stay here. His wife's about to have a baby.'

'Yeah, he did offer; he's feeling pretty guilty about the accident with the first cake. But I told him he should go home and that I'd do it. So…well, he's teaching me how to make icing-sugar roses.'

What? Now wasn't the time to mention that Craig made it look easy because he'd had years of practice.

'Okay… Well…that'll be okay.' Andrea searched her mind for something positive and encouraging to say. 'You're a surgeon, so you must be good with a knife.'

'A scalpel, actually…' He shot her an unconvinced look.

'Use a scalpel, then. There's a whole box of them up in the medical suite. Imagine… I don't know, imagine you're doing sutures.'

'Operation Cake, then.'

'Yes. Operation Cake.' Andrea caught sight of something in the ruins of the old cake. She picked it up, wiping it off. 'Look, the little statuette of the bride and groom is okay. We've still got that.'

Suddenly he caught her hand, pressing her fingers to his lips. That, more than anything else, made the panic subside. 'You think it'll work, then.'

'Yes, of course it'll work. We don't have any choice, do we? I'm not going to be the one to tell Maggie that she can't have a cake on her wedding day.'

'No. Me neither.'

'I'd better go back to the dinner. Maggie will get suspicious and come to find us if we're both AWOL. I'll come back here as soon as I can slip away and give you a hand.'

Cal shook his head. 'You'll be up all night. You've been working hard all day.'

'So have you. And it won't be the first time I've pulled an all-nighter. We can do this, Cal.'

He nodded quietly. The calm, cool-headed doctor was back. 'Okay. Thanks. I'll see you later, then. Even if you can just stay for an hour or so, that would be fantastic.'

Andrea put the little bride and groom statuette into his hand. She really wanted to stay here now, with Cal, but she had to cover for him at the dinner.

'I forgot the most important thing...' Andrea heard his voice behind her as she was turning to go.

'Yes?'

'You look beautiful tonight.'

CHAPTER ELEVEN

THE DINNER WAS AGONY. Despite her reassurances to Cal, Andrea was swallowing down her panic. Less than eighteen hours until the wedding and they had no cake.

Somehow, she got through the dinner. She told Maggie and Joe that Cal was arranging a last-minute surprise for the bridesmaids, which was close enough to the truth. This particular bridesmaid was going to be completely gobsmacked if they managed to produce something that even approximated a wedding cake, let alone compared with the beautiful cake that Maggie had chosen.

She took her leave as soon as she could. Then Andrea hurried back to her apartment, changing into a T-shirt and jeans and using the back stairs to go down to the kitchen so she wouldn't be seen.

Washing up was under way and the gleaming kitchen was being restored to its usual order for the morning. Cal was in one corner, wearing a borrowed chef's jacket and apron. Hopefully the cake was on course to be as delicious as he looked.

'Hey.' He gave her a smile. 'I didn't expect you so soon.'

'How's it going?' Andrea craned her head around him and saw a white sugar rose, placed carefully at the far end of his work station. 'That's the one Craig gave you as an example?'

'It's my first try...well, it's the fourth try, but this is the first one I didn't throw away. What do you think?' He surveyed the rose with a critical eye.

'You did that? It's brilliant, Cal.'

'Just another dozen to go, then.' He pointed at a sketch, tacked up on the tiled splashback. 'This is what we're aiming for.'

It was ambitious. A three-tiered cake, with a spray of leaves and roses snaking from top to bottom. There were butterflies amongst the leaves, and tiny roses around the statuette of the bride and groom.

'We're doing *that*? Isn't it a bit ambitious?'

'Craig showed me a few tricks for making the roses. They'll cover up the imperfections in the icing—that's the most difficult part to get right. He's left a list of all the things we need to do, and a diagram of where the support dowels go. That part actually looks quite easy…'

'You can do that, then. What can I do to help?'

Cal grinned. 'He left a jacket and apron for you. The cakes should be cool now so they need to be iced. There's a butterfly cutter just there, or I'll show you how to do the roses.'

'You stick with the roses; it looks as if you've mastered them now. I'll ice the cakes, shall I? I've plastered an old fireplace before…'

'Great. You have all the skills you need, then.' Cal's smile was enough to supply Andrea with the confidence she needed. 'Craig's left about a tonne of icing in those bowls over there, so we've got plenty to work with. I asked him to do some extra in case of mistakes.'

It looked as if Craig had anticipated more than a few mistakes. There was enough icing here to cover the whole ballroom. But now wasn't the time to be thinking about what could go wrong. Andrea fixed her gaze onto the sketch. If this went right, it would be beautiful.

Andrea picked up the apron, looping it over her head. 'Let's get started, then.'

Two o'clock in the morning. It was usually the lowest point in any long night, but Cal's presence had kept Andrea going. Always positive, always supportive. There was a line of roses now, of various different sizes, and he'd applied a dark pink blush to the pale pink ones. The icing on the cakes wasn't perfectly smooth but it would do, and Cal had carefully sunk the supporting dowels into the cakes and stacked them. Andrea's icing-sugar butterflies had turned out to be better than she expected and Cal had brought them to life with a few adept strokes of a fine brush, coated with food dye. Andrea stood back to survey their handiwork.

'You know, if ever we can't find work as doctors, speciality cakes might be an option.'

Cal chuckled, straightening his back and stretching. 'We could. Although this is surprisingly nerve-racking. I don't know how Craig stands the strain.'

'It's all a matter of what you know, isn't it?' Andrea suspected that Cal had put his surgical skills to use tonight: the care and the concentration; the exact precision of his work; his steady hand.

Cal nodded. 'I think that's it now. Just one more thing before we can start putting the roses onto the cake.'

'What's that?'

'The last one. We'll make it together.'

But...he was so good at them. And it would

be quicker if Cal did it himself. But he seemed determined that she should help.

'Yes. I'd really like that.'

She rolled out the icing, and Cal cut each layer of petals carefully to shape. Then it was a matter of teasing out the edges of each layer, so they would look like the delicate folds of a petal.

'Ah. No, that's no good.' Andrea discarded the rather odd-looking rose.

'Try again. Like this.' Cal cut another layer, nudging her fingers into just the right place as she made the tiny centre. 'Now you curl the petals out, thinning the edges. And you build up your rose from there.'

He was so close. So careful and precise. He guided her shaking fingers, his thumb pressing on hers to flatten the edges of each petal. Perfectly in unison, making something wonderful together.

'That's it. Beautiful.' His voice sounded quietly in her ear. 'Now we sign our work.'

He dipped the brush into the food dye, carefully inscribing a small 'C' on the back of the rose where it couldn't be seen. Then he handed Andrea the brush, and she made a wobbly 'A', right next to it.

'Cal…' Andrea set the rose down, turning to wrap her arms around him.

'Never thought we'd get this far?' He returned the hug.

'No.' She laid her head against his chest. The kitchen was still warm but nothing like as hot as it had been in the aftermath of the evening's cooking. His warmth seeped through her, making her feel strong and confident enough to finish what they'd started, and place the roses and butterflies on the cake according to the sketch.

'Me neither. But we're nearly there now...' He was gazing down at her. Nearly there suddenly seemed tantalisingly far away. Andrea stood on her toes, planting a kiss onto his jaw.

There was that sharp sigh that told her he wanted just the same as she did. And then his mouth on hers, soft as the touch of rose petals. Demanding, in the way that Cal did so well. She could feel her whole body responding to the kiss, her legs beginning to shake...

But he was there. Strong and solid. Holding her in his arms as if she was the most precious thing in the world. Kissing her as if that was the most beautiful thing in the world. Having to let him go was so very unfair.

And so very necessary. Amongst other things, they had a cake to finish.

'We'll be here when the morning shift comes

in to make breakfast at this rate.' It was Cal who broke the spell.

'Yes. Better get on...'

It was gone three o'clock but the cake was done. Cal carried it to the store room, giving it one last look before he covered it carefully. He couldn't believe they'd actually managed to produce something that looked vaguely like the sketch Craig had given him. They took off their aprons, making for the stairs together.

'I think I've got my second wind. I'm starting to feel wide awake.' Andrea smiled up at him when they reached the door of her apartment.

'Yes, me too. Must be relief. I didn't think we'd do as well as we have.'

'No, me neither. Would you like to come in for some hot chocolate?'

The hot chocolate he could take or leave. Another ten minutes with Andrea, before he went alone to his bed, seemed absolutely necessary. 'Yes. Thanks.'

When he sat down on the long, comfortable sofa, Cal realised his back was aching from bending over the countertop. Andrea disappeared into the kitchen, coming back with two steaming cups of chocolate. She sat down next to him.

This companionable silence was nice—warm and comfortable, and spiced with the knowledge that they'd taken on something that had seemed impossible, and somehow managed it. Andrea snuggled against him, and he felt his eyelids begin to droop...

Cal was warm and comfortable. It must be a dream because he could feel the soft weight of a woman, half on top of him. He knew it must be Andrea because she smelled of icing-sugar roses.

Cal's eyes snapped open. Andrea. Her sofa. Her apartment. In a moment of sudden panic, he tried to piece together their progress here, but he could only get as far as two cups of hot chocolate. Then he realised he was fully dressed and so was she.

They'd both been tired last night. He'd probably kicked off his shoes while still dreaming, and one or other of them had pulled the throw from the back of the sofa across them. But now he was awake and able to appreciate every breath she took—and each one of the moments that he could hold her sleeping body.

It was overwhelming. Cal wondered if it could have been any more perfect if they *had* made love last night.

Andrea moved slightly, and he saw her hand

move towards her face, as if to brush the sleep from her eyes. She was awake too. But he lay still, savouring these last moments of being able to hold her.

Then an alarm sounded in the bedroom. Andrea shifted, disentangling herself from his arms.

'You're awake, then.' She made no pretence of having been woken by the alarm.

'Yes. You too...'

She wasn't going to ask, and neither was he. Admitting that they'd both lain in each other's arms, not wanting to move, was a step too far for both of them. He swung his legs off the sofa, taking her with him as he sat up.

She scrubbed her hands across her head, obviously trying to tame her curls. He liked them just the way they were, along with the pinkness of her cheeks, and her sleepy eyes.

'I didn't realise I was so tired. I must have just sat down and fallen asleep.'

'Same here.' Cal didn't really want to talk about it. He didn't want to make excuses or pretend that nothing had happened. Something *had* happened, and this morning he felt so close to her. He didn't want to lose that feeling.

But it was slowly ebbing away anyway. Andrea walked into the bedroom to switch off the alarm, and then collected the untouched cups of chocolate.

'We're going to have to show Maggie the cake.' She plumped herself down in one of the easy chairs opposite him. So far away now.

'Yes. Probably best to get it over with as soon as possible. If she's really disappointed then you and Joe will have a chance to talk her round.'

'Don't think like that, Cal. I know it's not what she chose, but it's lovely. I'll have a shower then I'll go and get her; she'll be up by now. Meet you down in the kitchen in fifteen minutes?'

Cal made it down to the kitchen in ten. When he got there, Craig was in the store room, surveying the cake.

'What do you think? The icing looks great, doesn't it? Andrea did a good job with that.' Cal stared at it. In the cold light of day, he could see a couple of places where the rose petals weren't exactly right.

'Good effort, both of you. *Really* good effort.' Craig nodded his approval. 'I probably couldn't have done better myself.'

That was real praise. Cal felt the nagging worry lift slightly.

'Thanks. How's your wife?'

'Oh… We're still waiting. She woke me up

last night saying that she thought the baby might be coming, but it turned out to be…what do you call it?'

'Braxton Hicks? They usually stop if you change position, or move around a bit.'

'That's right. Braxton Hicks.' Craig wiped his hand across his face. 'The waiting's driving me crazy.'

'Babies have a habit of coming only when *they're* ready.'

Craig laughed. 'She's working to her own timetable all right. She's a strong little lass; I feel her kick sometimes when the wife's lying next to me in bed.'

A sudden burst of longing filled Cal's chest and he swallowed hard. 'That's good. It sounds as if everything's going as it should.'

'Yeah, yeah. The midwife's really pleased…' Craig broke off, looking through the open door. 'Here they are…'

Andrea was leading Joe and Maggie across the kitchen towards them. Cal stepped out of the store room, and Craig closed the door behind them.

'What are we all doing down here? We've already tasted everything on the menu…' Maggie was glowing. Andrea was hiding it well, but, despite her earlier reassurances, Cal could see something akin to terror in her eyes.

'There was a problem with the cake, Maggie. We've made you another one.' Andrea had obviously decided that it was necessary to give the bad news first, but that she should follow it up as quickly as possible with the good news.

But Maggie heard only the bad news. Her hand flew to her mouth and her eyes filled with tears.

'My cake? No!'

'It's all right, Maggie—' Andrea was almost pleading with her friend.

'Yes. Yes, it's all right.' Maggie turned to Joe, flinging her arms around him. 'We don't need cake, do we, Joe? We have each other...'

Joe was smiling. 'Seems we have cake as well. Didn't you hear Andrea say that they've made us another one?'

Maggie looked around the kitchen wildly. Andrea seemed paralysed with a mixture of hope and dread, and Cal decided he'd better do something. He opened the door of the store room, leading Maggie inside.

She stared at the cake. Everyone seemed to be holding their breath.

'You made a cake... For us... It's *beautiful*. Look, Joe. Better than the other one.' Maggie flung her arms around Cal, almost knocking him over, and then hugged Andrea.

'You're so clever. I didn't know you could make icing-sugar roses.'

Andrea finally smiled. 'I can't. I just did the icing. Craig baked the cake and made the icing, and Cal did the roses.'

'Cal! You're such a dark horse. Who'd have thought you could make roses? And, Craig, thank you so much.' A thought occurred to Maggie. 'So what happened to the other one?'

'One of the cooks fell down the stairs. He was carrying the cake.' Andrea volunteered the information.

'Oh! I hope he's all right?'

'Yes, he's fine. When Cal showed me what was left of the cake, it looked as if it had broken his fall.'

'That's just as well. I wouldn't have wanted him to be hurt and we couldn't wish for anything better than this, could we, Joe? Our friends making us this gorgeous cake.'

'No, we couldn't. Thank you both. And you, Craig.' Joe shook Craig's hand and then put his arm around Maggie. 'Is it okay with you if we go and get married now?'

CHAPTER TWELVE

IT WAS A beautiful ceremony. The huge auditorium had been cleared and decked with flowers, and Maggie and Joe both shone with happiness as they said their vows. Everyone's eyes were on the bride...except for Cal's. It was every bridesmaid's intention not to outshine the bride, but, in his eyes, Andrea just couldn't help it.

It was artifice of the very best kind. Andrea looked as if a passing cherub had sprinkled pearls into her hair, while another had wound soft tendrils of dusty pink satin around her body. Simple and yet immaculate, perfect in every way. He could have rested his gaze on the curve of her neck for hours.

She presided quietly over everything, giving a nudge here and a push there to smooth Maggie's path through the day. The three younger bridesmaids, wearing white lace dresses with pink sashes that matched Andrea's dress, were exactly where they should be without any apparent effort on Andrea's part. The guests moved into the ballroom, and the food was served. When the time came to make his speech, Andrea leaned towards him, her smile propelling him to his feet.

And then the moment he'd been waiting for. The toasts had been made, the tables cleared away. Maggie floated across the dance floor in Joe's arms, and even then Cal could only see Andrea.

'What's next?' He leaned over, whispering the words. They both knew exactly what came next.

'Oh… I'm not sure. Something to do with the best man, I think.'

'There's something I've forgotten?' Fat chance. Cal had been thinking about this all day.

'I can't for the life of me think what it is…' She gasped as he swung her onto the dance floor.

Two bodies moving in exact rhythm. There was nothing else, just the two of them, alone on a dance floor that was already full of other couples. She melted into his arms, finally letting go of the quiet watchfulness that had guided the day this far.

'You've done a wonderful job, Andrea. It's been a day to remember.'

'I couldn't have done it without you. Thank you, Cal.'

'I just followed the instructions in the folder.' He smiled down at her. 'You're the one who wrote them.'

She was silent for a moment, her cheek resting lightly against his chest. Cal wondered if silence would ever be the same again, when soon it would just be silence, without Andrea to share it. Without her to fill it with the sweetest things.

'I don't mean just the wedding. I'm not sure I could have done any of the last two weeks without you. I feel…different. Freer than I was.'

He felt different too. Cal allowed himself to wonder if that might be enough. If somehow they'd both managed to change and become entirely different people. The kinds of people who didn't have to part in a few days.

Even now, he couldn't see it. When Andrea was in his arms, almost anything seemed possible, but not the thing he really wanted.

'I'm glad.' It meant more to Cal than a wedding, more than anything they'd encountered in the last two weeks. One day, Andrea would be free of the ghosts that haunted her. Maybe not any time soon, but she'd taken the first step—wanting to be free instead of accepting that she never would be.

Time would tell. But time wasn't something they had at their disposal. Cal had to let go of her.

Not yet, though. Not while the music was still playing and he could hold her in his arms. Cal spread his fingers across her back, trying to take in every part of the sensation of having her close.

She wanted to keep Cal for herself, but that would be greedy, and the wedding folder itinerary dictated that he dance with a whole string of other people. Aunt Mae took her turn, looking gorgeous in a sequinned dress, and surprisingly light on her feet when she got onto the dance floor.

When it was time to cut the cake, Joe gave a little speech, just in case no one had heard about the catastrophe with the original cake yet. Then Maggie squealed with delight as skiers with flaming torches traversed the slopes outside in a complicated fire dance, which ended with torches being stuck into the snow outside in the shape of a heart.

Craig handed Joe a shining silver knife, and he and Maggie made the first cut, then insisted on Andrea and Cal making the second. She felt his fingers curl around hers, and the applause was just as enthusiastic as it had been for Joe and Maggie.

Despite Craig's insistence that Maggie leave all this to him, she made sure that a large piece was wrapped carefully for Craig to take home to his wife. And somehow, the rose that bore their initials found its way onto Andrea's plate.

'I can't bring myself to eat it.' She pulled a face. She couldn't bring herself not to eat it either, because she couldn't keep it. It would crack and fade, and become a worn-out memory of something that should stay fresh for ever.

'It was made to be enjoyed.'

That was always Cal's response. Live for the here and now, not the past and maybe not the future. Andrea broke off a couple of the petals, putting them onto his plate.

'Will you help me with it, then?'

Their rose. Eaten together at the wedding that they had helped to create. It seemed to seal an unspoken promise between them, just as much as the spoken promises that Joe and Maggie had made.

Suddenly, it was a little too much to bear. Andrea turned away from him, finding that one of the bridesmaids was about to smear chocolate cake all over her dress, and that the little girl's face required a quick wipe with a paper napkin. When she glanced at Cal again, he was eating the sugar petals, his gaze still fixed on her.

Something had to be done about this. She had to make a decision, one way or the other, and stick by it.

The world wouldn't stop changing just because she wanted it to.

It was time to reach out and take it by the scruff of the neck.

Andrea heaved a sigh of relief as Joe and Maggie left the reception, bound for their suite. The party was beginning to break up, and if any stragglers decided they wanted to make a night of it, the hotel staff would deal with that. She took a deep breath and walked over to where Cal was standing. He still looked as handsome as he had this morning and just as immaculate, seemingly untouched by the rigours of avoiding champagne spills on his jacket, icing sugar on his tie, and the creasing effect that an evening's dancing could have on a shirt.

First step: get him alone.

'Would you like a nightcap? Hot chocolate instead of champagne? I promise to stay awake this time.'

He nodded. 'I could definitely sit down and relax for a moment. Chocolate would be nice, too.'

Second step: back to her apartment and kick off her shoes.

That was a relief. Andrea padded into the kitchen to make the hot chocolate, and Cal took off his jacket and loosened his tie, lowering himself onto the sofa.

He looked even more delicious now. That, and the knowledge that Cal would never hurt her, made the third step laughably easy.

'A lot's happened in the last two weeks...' Andrea sat next to him on the sofa, taking a sip of her chocolate.

'Yeah. It's been...' He twisted his mouth in a wry smile. 'I wouldn't exactly say it's all been fun. But it's been good. And a lot more than just special.'

So he felt the way she did. If she'd stopped to think for a moment she would have known that already. She also knew that Cal would never ask. He'd made an agreement with her and he would respect that, however much they both wanted to change it now.

'I want you to stay tonight.' Six words. So very quick and easy to say, but once they were out she couldn't take them back. There was no uncertainty, no ambiguity to hide behind.

His face hardened suddenly. 'I…can't, Andrea. It's not that I don't want to, but you said it yourself. You don't need anyone in your life, right now.'

He was hiding something. She'd been honest with him, and if he could give her nothing else then he could return that favour.

'You're telling me what I need? If I didn't know you better, I'd say that was a little arrogant.'

He held up his hands in a gesture of surrender. 'No. I'm sorry, I didn't mean it that way. But I'm going home in two days and…we have very different lives. I can't just take what I want and then leave you behind. We both know that's what will happen. I'm the kind of person who thinks twice about taking a job I really want just because it wasn't my idea.'

She'd thought about that. And she was okay with it.

'So what's wrong with knowing it, and accepting it? Taking what we're both able to take?'

For a moment she thought he was going to forget all about his reservations and kiss her. If he did, she knew there would be no going back this time. But then the bright possibilities of a whole night spent together faded from his eyes.

'I'm not…' He shook his head. Leaning forward, and planting his elbows on his knees, he seemed to be studying the pattern on the carpet.

Andrea laid her hand on his shoulder. Whatever this was, she was here for him, the way he'd been there for her. But as soon as she touched him he flinched, and she snatched her hand away again.

'Andrea, I'm sorry…' He turned, catching her hand in his. 'I didn't mean…'

'What *do* you mean, Cal?' she chided him gently. 'Come on. Out with it.'

One side of his lip curled suddenly, in a lop-sided smile. 'I guess I deserve that.'

'You absolutely do.'

He let out a sigh, leaning back against the sofa cushions. Now the ceiling seemed to be the object of his full attention. Andrea waited.

'It took me a long time to achieve my ambitions. Even longer to come to terms with it and feel comfortable with what I wanted out of life.'

'I know.' Andrea wasn't sure what that had to do with anything at the moment.

'You're not ready to change either, are you?'

'No, but… Look, we made an agreement that we weren't going to get involved, Cal. We can keep to that, can't we?'

'And what happens if we can't?'

Andrea swallowed hard. She'd been trying not to think about that. Today had spun a magical web around them, but she could feel its tendrils loosening now. She reached for his hand before the spell was completely broken, and even now his fingers curled around hers in the instinctive reaction that happened between them every time.

'I hurt someone, Andrea. Badly.'

'What?' The idea that Cal would knowingly hurt anyone was ridiculous. But he was only human, and who could truthfully say that they'd never—even unwittingly—hurt someone?

'I was reckless, believing I could have things all my own way, and that the usual rules didn't apply to me. Mary's a good person, and she was a good friend. I told myself that it was possible to have a relationship with her, without letting it touch any other part of my life.'

'Did she know that was what you wanted?'

'It was her idea. Mary had the same kind of work commitments I did; she was a civil rights lawyer and she cared about the people who came to her for help. She worked hard and we both thought that a no-strings affair between friends would suit us.'

Something cold began to form in the pit of

Andrea's stomach. That was pretty much what she'd suggested to Cal.

'She fell in love. Mary had that option—she could compromise and let her work fit around the rest of her life for a while. I couldn't even contemplate it, and that's what hurt her the most.'

'This isn't the same, Cal.' She spoke without thinking, talking from the part of her that wanted him more than anything else.

He stared at her for a moment, and then shook his head. 'Your place is here, Andrea. Mine isn't. It's my heart and yours we're talking about, not a cake. If they break, we can't just whip another one up by the morning.'

Suddenly she was angry. Angry at all the things that had pulled them together, and all the things that kept them apart. Angry with Cal, because she suspected he was right, that they couldn't just walk away from each other after spending a night together.

'They don't *have* to break…'

He studied her face. 'Don't tell me you can do this, Andrea. I can't and I know you can't either.'

'I guess you should leave, then.' Her words came out cross and hurt instead of understanding and regretful, and when he got to his feet, catching up his jacket, she didn't stop him.

There wasn't any point in stopping him, because he really did need to go before something persuaded him to forget about that wretched honourable streak of his.

The latch on the door locked shut with a click. That was okay, because it meant he wouldn't be coming back. And if she had to be alone tonight, crying bitter tears into her pillow, then she might as well get on with it. Bring it on.

CHAPTER THIRTEEN

THE RESTAURANT, THE breakfast bar, and the covered veranda, where space heaters made it warm enough to sit and drink piping hot coffee, were still deserted. No one was up and about yet, and it looked as if most of the wedding guests had decided that brunch was a better option than breakfast.

Maggie had knocked on the door of Andrea's apartment this morning, asking if she wanted to come for coffee with her. Joe had gone out for a walk with his grandfather, who was anxious to impart the secret of a long and happy marriage.

'I suppose if anyone's going to know it would be Joe's grandpa. His grandparents have been married for nearly sixty years, without so much as a cross word.'

'Really? Isn't that a little bit boring?' Andrea wasn't in the mood to hear about domestic harmony this morning. Last night had been full of every kind of regret imaginable.

Maggie chuckled dryly. 'I don't think it's actually true. Joe's mum told me they've definitely been known to argue. They just keep it between themselves and work things out together.'

'Not such a bad approach.' Andrea should take a leaf from their book. She'd already decided to keep what had happened between her and Cal to herself. It would be a shame to cast any shadow over Maggie's obvious happiness, however much Andrea needed her friend right now.

'Yes, it sounds good to me too. Although Grandpa Dave's a bit late with the advice on how Joe can make me happy, because he's already done that. I think he just wants to go for a walk with Joe; they've always been close.'

'So…where shall we go?'

Maggie surveyed the display of food on the counter of the breakfast bar. 'Are you hungry? Joe and I already ate so I just want coffee.'

'That's all I want.' Andrea didn't even want to think about food at the moment.

'How about the veranda, then? Unless it's too cold for you?'

'No, it's fine.' Andrea had woken in the night, shivering, unable to get warm, even though she'd gone and sat in front of the fire in the sitting room. The crisp cold of the morning was nothing compared to the icy fingers of regret over things she ought to be able to change, but couldn't. And they'd be less likely to run into Cal on the veranda.

They sat down, arranging rugs over their legs. The waiter brought mugs of coffee and Maggie let out a contented sigh. 'It's so beautiful here. And you… You've done so much, Andrea. Thank you.'

'I've enjoyed it too. It's been a wonderful time.' That at least was true. It was over now, but it had been wonderful.

'Andrea?' Maggie set her mug down, grabbing Andrea's hand. It was only then that Andrea realised her eyes were full of tears. 'What's the matter, honey?'

'Nothing… I mean…' Andrea wiped the tears away with the sleeve of her sweater. 'It's just been so great to have you here. I'll miss you.'

'Are you sure that's all it is?' Maggie squeezed her hand. 'Did anything happen?'

Did anything happen with Cal? That was what Maggie meant; she wasn't blind. It was impossible to miss the chemistry between her and Cal.

'Nothing happened. And everything's fine, truly. I'm just a little tired.'

'Because you and Cal stayed up so late, making our cake.' Maggie smiled at her, leaning over for a hug. 'You're the best friend that anyone could have, Andrea.'

Maggie and Joe were leaving this afternoon for a week in the sunshine. Just six hours, and then Andrea could drop all the pretence and go and lock herself away in her apartment, until Cal left the hotel.

But there were still the goodbyes to get through. It was impossible that she shouldn't be there to wave her friends off, and if she knew Cal at all then he'd be thinking the same. At least she could position herself on the opposite side of the gaggle of friends and family, while Maggie and Joe worked their way round, kissing cheeks and shaking hands.

'We have to have a photo…' Maggie's mother had brought her camera with her. 'Andrea, go and stand next to Joe. And where's Cal?'

She could see the tension in Cal's face when he stepped forward. He took his place by Maggie's side, smiling for the camera. Andrea wondered if her own smile looked as pasted on as his did, but no one seemed to notice. Maggie's

mother fiddled with her camera, taking photograph after photograph.

'That'll be enough, Mum, surely.' Maggie
stepped forward, grinning, and took the camera from her mother. 'What about one with just
Andrea and Cal?'

The relief at the ordeal almost being over
was tempered by the knowledge that the worst
was still to come. Joe ducked out from between
them, and she felt Cal put his arm around her.

He could hardly touch her. Cal was doing
all the right things, standing next to her and
smiling for the camera, but his hand wasn't so
much on her shoulder as hovering a millime-
tre above it. Andrea smiled, unable to move
under the weight of numb misery.

As soon as Maggie had taken the photograph, he was gone. Maybe he had nothing
to say to her, or maybe he too was taking
Grandpa Dave's approach and keeping their
argument between themselves alone. Andrea
silently sent up a sigh of relief as Maggie and
Joe climbed onto the train, waving.

She could see Cal waving too, but as soon
as the train drew away, he turned to Grandpa
Dave. As the two walked away together,
Grandpa Dave seemed to be giving Cal the
benefit of his experience on something or other
and Cal was nodding gravely.

That was it, then. After all the excitement and the hubbub, the only thing that remained was for everyone to go home. Then, finally, Andrea could grieve, for the loss of the future that had seemed to open up before her and which she'd been too afraid to grab hold of.

Cal had done everything that was expected of him. He'd spent the night trying to get a few hours' sleep, but it had slipped through his fingers, as if it were playing a game of tag with him. Then he'd downed three cups of coffee, which had only served to leave him feeling like an overstretched piece of piano wire, before turning his mind to tackling the day.

He doggedly made the rounds of all the hotel staff who'd helped with the wedding, thanking each one personally. Somehow he managed to avoid Andrea, and he couldn't help wondering if it was because she was also avoiding him.

When the time came to see Maggie and Joe off, she couldn't even meet his gaze. Last night hadn't been an aberration or a misunderstanding between friends. It had shown them both that they could never be together.

A call to the airline secured a ticket home for this evening in exchange for the one he'd booked in two days' time. Cal packed his bags, walking down to the railway terminus. As the train drew into the station, the impulse to run back and try and make things right with Andrea seized him.

But things *were* right. He should never have allowed their relationship to go as far as it had, and he had no excuse other than having been dazzled by her. Andrea had found peace here, and if he loved her at all, then he should leave.

He picked up his bags and stepped into the carriage of the funicular train. As it drew away from the lights of the hotel, he didn't allow himself to look back.

Four days. It had been four days since Cal had left without a word. Andrea had been angry with him, and then angry at herself. Now she just felt numb.

But she had to keep going. She kept on smiling for the family and friends who were still at the hotel for a few days' holiday after the wedding. And kept on crying when she was alone.

She was woken by the doorbell. Sleeping late wasn't her usual habit—the mornings were far too crisp and beautiful for that—but she was exhausted from nights of staring at the ceiling, wondering how she'd managed to be so stupid as to lose Cal. He'd *told* her how he felt. They'd agreed that they wouldn't act on their feelings. She could have waved him off, knowing he'd be a friend she could contact any time she liked, but she'd destroyed all of that.

Aunt Mae was standing at the door of her apartment. She wore one of the hotel's Ski Mavericks bright pink sweatshirts over immaculate cream trousers and a polo neck.

'Aunt Mae. Come in.' Andrea wondered for a moment if she was still dreaming, and decided she wasn't. She'd arranged for Francine to take Aunt Mae for a ride on the slopes on one of the skidoos; Aunt Mae had obviously enjoyed herself and wanted a souvenir of the trip.

'You look as if you need something to start your day.' Aunt Mae walked determinedly into the small sitting room and sat down.

'Uh. Yes. I'm just going to make coffee. Would you like some?'

A visit from Aunt Mae always required that cups and saucers be used. Andrea combed her hair in the kitchen while she was waiting for the coffee to brew, and when she returned to the sitting room she found Aunt Mae emptying the contents of her handbag onto the coffee table, presumably looking for a sandwich.

'Would you like some toast?' Andrea set the cups down.

'No, I had breakfast some time ago. Don't let me stop you though, dear.'

'That's okay. I'm not hungry.' The bread in the kitchen was stale anyway.

Aunt Mae found what she was looking for and started to tip everything else back into her handbag. Andrea focussed on a small bottle of whisky, which must have come from the mini-bar in Aunt Mae's room.

'It's a bit early, isn't it?'

'Needs must, dear.' Aunt Mae opened the bottle, tipping a measure into both cups.

Andrea shrugged. 'Okay.' She obediently took a sip of her coffee, blinking from the taste of caffeine with alcohol. Maybe one sip was enough for courtesy's sake.

'Cal's very handsome, isn't he? He's got that sparkle I like in a man.'

So *this* was what Mae was here for. Not much got past her, and she must have seen what Andrea had been trying so hard to conceal. She'd obviously decided that Andrea needed a pick-me-up and that fortifying her coffee at ten-thirty in the morning was going to do the trick.

'Yes, he has. It's okay, Aunt Mae. I'm not going to fall to pieces.'

Aunt Mae reached into the neck of her sweatshirt, pulling out the old-fashioned locket that she always wore, and lifting the chain over her white, perfectly coiffed curls. 'I don't think I've ever shown you this, have I?'

'No, you haven't.' The locket was heavy in Andrea's hand. 'May I look inside?'

Aunt Mae nodded, and Andrea opened the locket. On one side was the picture of a young man in an army cap. On the other, an older man with a jovial smile.

'My two husbands.'

What? 'I didn't know you were married, Aunt Mae.'

'I haven't always been eighty, dear. I married Ted, the one on the right, when I was eighteen, just before he went away to do his National Service. He was killed, making me a widow at nineteen.'

Andrea caught her breath. Suddenly her own troubles seemed very small. 'I'm so sorry, Aunt Mae.'

'It was a long time ago, dear, and, as you know, time heals. I married my second husband, Harry, ten years later. We had twenty good years together, before he died of a heart attack.'

Andrea stared at Aunt Mae dumbly. Aunt Mae never failed to surprise, but she was pulling out all the stops this morning.

'It's… Aunt Mae, I never knew…' Andrea moved over to the sofa, giving Aunt Mae a hug.

'It's all right, dear. I loved them both and I'm thankful for every moment I had with each of them.' Aunt Mae extricated herself from Andrea's embrace. 'Harry was a tiger between the sheets, you know.'

'Aunt Mae!'

'You think you invented sex? You're not twelve years old any more, dear, and I assume you have a good idea about what I mean. Cal has that same something about him as my Harry did.'

Okay. Andrea definitely needed a drink now. She took a gulp of her coffee, blinking as it hit the back of her throat.

'We…um. We didn't ever get that far.'

Aunt Mae shot her a derisive look. 'In those days we didn't live together before we got married. But I knew exactly what to expect with my Harry, and he didn't disappoint.'

Andrea picked up the locket from the coffee table, gently fixing the chain back around Aunt Mae's neck. The worn engraving glinted in the sunlight, a testament to memories that had become mellow with age.

'Whisky at ten-thirty in the morning, and telling me you had two husbands. This isn't just a social call, is it, Aunt Mae? What is it you came to say?'

'I've had a good life, and I don't regret anything that I did. A few things that I didn't do, maybe...' Aunt Mae took a sip of her coffee, pausing as if to make a list in her head of the things she hadn't done. Clearly that wasn't relevant to her point.

'Live your life, Andrea. Take it from me: if you don't try for what you want you'll always regret it.'

'But... It's complicated. He doesn't want me...'

Aunt Mae snorted in disbelief. 'It's always complicated. In my experience, men are full of complications of one kind or the other. But they don't dance that way with women they don't want.'

Andrea felt a tear form at the corner of her eye. Aunt Mae had voiced the feeling that had been growing over the last few days, and suddenly it didn't seem so outrageous after all.

'Thank you...' She hugged Aunt Mae again, feeling the tears begin to flow down her cheeks. 'Thank you for...everything.'

'My pleasure, dear. There isn't much point in being this old if you can't dispense a little wisdom from time to time. Now, drink your coffee and go and get dressed. There's a little errand I want you to run for me.'

'What is it?' Andrea grinned, wiping her eyes. 'If you don't ask, then you don't get.'

'I'm glad you've been listening. Those torch processions they do at dusk...' Aunt Mae patted the design on her Ski Mavericks sweatshirt.

Andrea nodded. 'You want to be a part of one?'

'They *do* look rather exciting.'

'Consider it done. I'll come with you and take some pictures, shall I?' Andrea was sure that Francine and Bruno would be eager to make the occasion special, and that her parents would be there too, ready to celebrate Aunt Mae's intrepid zest for life when she reached the bottom of the slope.

Aunt Mae clapped her hands together. 'That would be lovely, thank you. Something to show everyone at the library, when I get home...'

'So how's married life, then?' Cal put two pints of best bitter down onto the table in the cosy 'snug' bar of Joe's local pub.

'Good. I'd recommend it.' Joe picked up his glass. 'Cheers.'

It was good to see Joe so happy. It took some of the edge off Cal's own unhappiness, making him feel that the world hadn't completely faded into grey.

'How are things with you? You said you'd taken the job you were offered?'

Cal nodded. 'The board of directors offered

me a great deal. We agreed that I'll be a relatively free agent for the next couple of months, working with the other directors to create new strategies for innovation. Then I'll take up my new role as London Director and start implementing some of those strategies.'

'Sounds great. You got over whatever it was that was giving you the heebie-jeebies about it?'

A vision of Andrea's smile formed in Cal's imagination. She'd been following him for a while now—all the way back from Italy, in fact. Cal sent a silent thank-you to her and hoped that whatever she was doing this evening brought her happiness. It was the only thing that justified the pain that, for the last two weeks, had sometimes seemed to be tearing his heart from his chest.

'Yeah. I took some good advice.'

Joe raised his eyebrows. 'That's new. Since when did you listen to anything anyone else had to say about your career?'

Since Andrea. It was as if everything had stopped when he'd met her, and then started anew.

'People change.'

'Yeah. I wouldn't disagree with you there.' Joe reached forward, picking up his beer. 'I just didn't think I'd ever hear *you* say it.'

Cal shrugged. 'Like I say, people change.'

Joe narrowed his eyes. 'Am I missing something? You could sound a lot more enthusiastic about this.'

His friend hadn't missed anything. It was hard to keep up a positive façade when he felt his heart was breaking—a slow-motion disintegration that robbed Cal daily of even the smallest pleasures.

'You remember when you told me that you'd met the woman you wanted to marry?' Cal took a sip of his beer, the taste sour in his mouth.

'Of course I do…' Understanding dawned in Joe's face. 'Ah. Andrea.'

'Was it *that* obvious?'

'Put it like this: I haven't witnessed that much chemistry since I was at school, doing my science A levels. You've told her?'

Cal shook his head. 'You know as well as I do that Andrea's vulnerable. She has her own comfort zone and she's happy there. She doesn't need me crashing into her life.'

Joe thought for a moment. 'You're sure about that? A good friend once told me that if I loved Maggie, then I shouldn't let her go so easily.'

'That's different. You're not an uncompromising control freak.'

'She said *that* about you?' Joe raised his eyebrows.

'No, actually. She doesn't know me quite as well as you do. You've said it a few times.'

'Only in jest…' Joe shrugged, but he knew it was true, just as well as Cal did.

Somehow, though, Andrea was still here: sitting at his elbow, telling him that he could change; believing in him the way he believed in her. The distant possibility that maybe one day they could both change, and that they'd be together, was all that kept him going at the moment.

'Look, Cal. I know this is hard, but… If you really love her, isn't it better to face the obstacles together?'

Cal shook his head. 'You and Maggie are different. You weren't the obstacle, were you?'

Joe grumbled into his beer, but he couldn't disagree. Cal didn't want to talk about it any more, and he walked over to the deep window ledge, sorting out the chess men from the pile of different board games, and setting them out on the chequered table between him and Joe.

The black-hearted king, who loved a glimmering white queen. Cal's very nature made it impossible. But some impossible things were just harder and took longer. He had nothing left but a distant, unreachable hope and, despite everything his head was telling him, his instinct was to cling to it.

Joe rubbed his hands together, flexing his fingers in preparation for the battle ahead.

CHAPTER FOURTEEN

One week later

'ANDREA…?' FOR ONE split second Cal looked as if he'd seen a ghost. But he'd always been able to think on his feet. 'It's nice to see you.'

'It's good to see you too, Cal.'

He stepped back from the doorway, beckoning her inside. 'You're in London to see Maggie and Joe?'

'No, I flew in this morning. I'm on my way up to Oxford. I thought I'd surprise my mum and dad with a visit. Maybe drop in on Aunt Mae.'

The excuse seemed thin at best but Cal accepted it without a murmur. He was a perfect facsimile of someone who'd opened the door and found an old friend standing on his front step. Andrea saw straight through him.

'I was just about to make some tea…' He hadn't offered to take her coat and Andrea assumed he was hoping she wouldn't stay long enough for tea.

'Tea would be really nice. Thank you.'

He nodded, leading her to the back of the hallway and into the kitchen. Andrea bit back the urge to shake him. Surely he couldn't keep this up for much longer. He was smiling, but the dark rings under his eyes told a different story.

'I'm beginning to wonder whether I've done the right thing.'

He flipped the kettle on, feigning a questioning look. 'How so?'

'Because the Cal Lewis I know is a darn sight more honest than this.'

He was doing exactly what she'd been doing for the last three weeks. Pasting on a smile and pretending that nothing had happened, even though she knew that she'd always regret losing Cal.

He was suddenly still, staring at her silently. Andrea could almost hear her own heart beating furiously in her chest. If he didn't say something…anything…she was going to lose it and burst into tears. That, or threaten him with one of those fancy frying pans that hung over the large, gleaming hob.

'What are you doing here, Andrea?' There

was a look of such anguish in his eyes that she forgave him everything.

'I came to talk to you, Cal. I *need* to talk to you.'

He shook his head, slowly. 'Is there anything left to say, Andrea? We can't do this.'

That was all part of the problem—this fantasy that they hadn't gone all the way and that it was possible to draw back without any loss. Somehow, in the space of two weeks, they'd got in so deep that the only way out was to work their way through to the other side.

And then…she had to convince Cal that she didn't *want* out. And find out whether he felt the same.

She walked across the kitchen to where he was standing. Facing him down. There was nowhere for him to go; his back was already against the sleek grey counter top.

He could smile. He could pretend he felt nothing, but his body told the truth. Cal couldn't control the sudden dilation of his eyes, the pulse that beat wildly at the side of his neck. They were both doctors, trained to see these things, and he could probably see it in her too. The way her whole body was screaming for him even though they weren't touching.

'How does this make you feel, Cal?' She

held his gaze steadily, knowing he was helpless to tear himself away.

'It makes me feel…too many things.'

'Me too.'

He reached out, his fingers following the curve of her cheek. Cal didn't even touch her, but she could feel her skin begin to heat.

'I can't deny what we have, Andrea. That's the reason I left, because I can't resist it.'

She nodded. Now that he was being honest, she should be too.

'I let you leave because I was angry with you. And then I missed you, and then, when I got my head straight and thought about things a little more, I was angry with myself. Then I just missed you again.'

He smiled suddenly. Not the controlled smile he'd been wearing before, but something that came from deep inside. Seeing it again made Andrea tremble.

'I guess it's a pretty standard process.' The kettle began to boil and switched itself off with a snap. He didn't even look at it, but shot her an apologetic look. 'Tea…?'

'Yes.' Andrea needed to break the tension too. Her head was beginning to swim, and her knees were starting to shake. She nodded, moving away from him.

But they'd broken through. No more pretending that this wasn't happening, and no more hiding from it. As with everything else, it had taken far less time than Andrea could have imagined.

She watched him as he made the tea. He seemed to feel her gaze, turning to smile at her. Then, picking up the cups, he walked through to a large sitting room, perching them on the end of a large coffee table that was stacked with books and papers.

'I interrupted you. You're working.' Cal had obviously been using his Saturday morning to catch up on some paperwork.

He eyed the pile thoughtfully. Then, suddenly, in a broad sweep of movement that took her breath away, he cleared it all to one side, tipping it onto the floor.

'Not any more.'

It was the only thing he could think of in the heart-stopping moment he'd seen Andrea on his doorstep. Act normal, and pretend he'd bumped into an old friend with whom he'd shared a few might-haves. But he'd seen the look in Andrea's eyes right from the start, and it was impossible to keep the sham up.

She had his full attention. He'd tried filling his thoughts with as many other things as he could, and all that had done was exhaust him.

Andrea had always had his full attention, from the very first moment he'd seen her.

Andrea sat at one end of the sofa and Cal sat at the other. Now that she was a little further away from him, he could at least think of something other than the madness of having her close. The madness of wanting her close, maybe...

'Andrea, this thing we have...' He wasn't explaining himself very well but she nodded in understanding. 'It'll destroy us both if we let it.'

'How so?'

So she wanted him to say it. Out loud. At this moment he'd do anything she asked.

'You've made a life for yourself again, and found a place where you can heal. I want to tell you that I can give you everything you need to heal, but... I can try my best, but if that's not good enough...' It would break both their hearts. His didn't matter, but Andrea's was precious beyond measure.

Her eyes softened, and the pain of knowing that he would lose her all over again was almost unbearable.

'Cal, I know you don't want to hurt me. I came here to tell you that you can't. I told you that the mountains were my happy place, and they were. But you've helped me move on from that. My happy place is with you.'

He still couldn't believe it. Didn't dare believe it. The stakes were too high.

'You can't know that, Andrea. We were together for two weeks, and we never even…' He couldn't say it. But she held his gaze, even if her cheeks were beginning to flush.

'We never even slept together?'

'No.' Only in his head, and quite obviously in hers too. 'We hardly know each other.'

'I know everything I need to know about you, Cal. You're the man I've been looking for, and I love you. Everything else is just…' she waved her hand dismissively '…details.'

'I wouldn't have called it *just details*.' He grinned at her. Andrea was smiling too.

'Attention to detail is always a good thing.'

'Yes, it is. Always.'

She loved him. Cal couldn't tear his thoughts away from that particular detail, because he loved Andrea too. Completely and unreservedly.

Suddenly, he knew. Cal could do anything if Andrea was by his side, guiding him. The one piece of the puzzle that held all of the answers was sitting here beside him. Andrea had given him another chance, and he couldn't let it go.

'I think…' She took an unsteady breath. 'We probably need some time to think about this.'

'You mean *I* do?' Cal had spent far too much time thinking about this, and the answer was clear. He knew now exactly what he'd be doing with the rest of his life.

'I have rather sprung this on you.'

He reached for her, taking her hands between his. 'Andrea, I love you. If you know an answer to this, a way we can be together… please tell me.'

She flushed, suddenly. 'I don't have all the answers. But I trust you and I think that if you trust me back then there's nothing we can't do together.'

'I trust you enough to believe you. Do you trust me enough to allow me to kiss you?'

Her eyes darkened in delicious welcome. 'Yes.'

They'd stayed in the moment for a long time, exploring every facet of it, sharing each beat of their hearts. When Cal took her in his arms, carrying her into the bedroom, the next moment began to unfold before her.

He was tender, and yet passionate. He undressed her slowly, not allowing her to lose sight of the bright promise of what was to come.

'Cal, I…' As he slipped her blouse off, his

kisses moving from her neck to her shoulder, she felt suddenly embarrassed and clung to him for comfort.

'Tell me.' He folded her in his arms.

She'd never minded her scars. Most had faded, and were almost invisible now, but the two on her shoulder were still evident and always would be. And suddenly they seemed to matter, because Cal was so perfect. So flawless.

'My shoulder is… I never really looked at it before and it didn't seem to matter. Now I don't think it looks so nice.' Perhaps he could concentrate on kissing the other one.

He sat down on the bed, taking her in his lap. 'You're the most beautiful woman I've ever seen, Andrea. I could tell you that the scars don't matter, but they do. They matter because every part of you matters. I want to be here for you as you reclaim yourself.'

He understood. Now everything seemed to matter just that bit more, because she'd started to care again. But Cal wouldn't let her down. He'd be there to help her recover every part of her life.

She kissed him, cradling his face in her hands. Passion didn't lie and she knew he found her beautiful.

'You'll be here with me?' He asked.

'Always. I won't let you get away with any-thing, Cal. We'll bend together…'

He smiled. 'I can't think of anything I want more. Bending with you in a warm breeze and building our future. I love you, Andrea.'

She kissed him, whispering her agreement against his cheek. She wanted everything that Cal's love could give her. They took their plea-sure slowly, exploring every part of each oth-er's bodies, until finally they could take no more. Cal tipped her onto her back, holding her tight as she wrapped her legs around his waist.

There was a moment of sweet, still silence. Then he whispered her name as he slowly pushed inside her, and she felt her own body welcoming his in a yearning embrace.

He was still again, kissing her tenderly. Tell-ing her how much he'd wanted this, and that he'd loved her from the first moment he saw her.

And then the passion began to rise between them. There was no hesitation, and no uncer-tainty. No limits.

She was home. Finally home.

Andrea lay tangled in his arms as the first light of morning slanted through the window.

'One thing I didn't know about you…' She caressed his cheek and his eyes opened.

'Hmm? What's that?'

'All those fantasies. They weren't as good as the real thing.'

Cal grinned sleepily. 'You had fantasies? That's nice. I think I'll be fantasising about you fantasising about me.'

'All the time.' There wasn't a single thing she couldn't tell him, and nothing she couldn't ask, either. 'What about you?'

'Just the one. It started about ten seconds after I met you. And lasted until yesterday morning. Then you made it all real.' He gave her a broad, contented smile. 'Several times.' He chuckled. 'Reality's good. I can take a great deal more of it.'

'Just as well that I happen to be free, then.'

He stretched luxuriously, propping himself up on one elbow. 'Italy or London. What do you think?'

Andrea had already made up her mind. 'London. Definitely.'

'You're sure? I was thinking how much I liked the mountains.'

'Your job's here, Cal.'

'Everything's up for grabs, Andrea. Everything apart from us being together, that is.' He grinned at her.

Cal would have left his job behind, everything he'd built, to be with her. And Andrea knew he'd do it without looking back; he'd made it clear that his happy place was with her, just as hers was with him.

'The Alps will always be there for us whenever we want, Cal. But I want to come back home and live in London. I've been away too long already, and there's a lot I still want to do.'

'If that's what you really want—'

Andrea silenced him with a kiss. That settled the question.

'All right. I hear you. London it is. I do have one condition, though.'

'What's that?'

'I told the board of directors at the clinic that I'd take the job they were offering. It means working from home for a few months, and that's an opportunity to come out to Italy with you for a while. We won't rush back, we'll take our time over it.'

'But, Cal…you know I believe in the work you do. It's important. If you need to be here in London I'll join you as soon as I can…'

He put his finger lightly on her lips. 'We belong together and it only takes a little flexibility to make that happen. I'll be needing to talk to a lot of people, based in various different places, and I can do that from Italy just as well as I can from here.'

'You're sure?'

'I'll need your support, and I'll be asking you for some ideas, too. You have experience of overhauling systems so that everything's working in the best way possible.'

'You have my support, always.' She reached up, winding her arms around his neck. 'Now that we know where we're going to live, and what you're going to do, the only thing left is for us to find something for me to do. We can think about that later, though…'

'Yeah? What do you have in mind in the meantime?' Cal grinned. His body was already responding to the pressure of hers as she pulled him close.

'I'm overhauling our own personal system. Establishing a precedent for lazy Sunday mornings in bed.'

'That sounds like an interesting concept. I think we should explore it a little more fully…'

It had been the best weekend of his life. He'd taken Andrea to the airport early on Monday morning, promising that he'd be in Italy on Friday evening. Then he'd gone into work, and outlined his plans to the other directors, who had given him their full support.

Everything was coming together. Andrea had called him, saying she'd given in her notice at the hotel, and told them she'd stay on for a couple of months to ensure a smooth handover. That evening he'd called Joe.

'Joe, I want to ask a favour.'

'Sure.'

'You know I told you that I'd met the woman I want to marry…'

'Yeah?' A note of caution sounded in Joe's voice.

'Well, it appears that Andrea's crazy enough to want to spend some time with me. I need your help with something.'

Joe's delighted chuckle sounded in his ear. 'What do you need, mate?'

She was waiting on the platform as the funicular drew into the hotel terminus. Cal waited impatiently for the doors to open, and as soon as they did Andrea flung herself into his arms, almost squashing the roses he'd bought for her.

It felt like an age since he'd touched her. He told her how much he'd missed her and she whispered that they'd make up for that tonight. But first they'd eat; he must be famished.

They had dinner in the restaurant, at Andrea's favourite table, the one by the window.

'You'll miss this, when we're back in London.' Cal looked out at the dark shapes of the mountains, under a sky bright with stars.

'A little. Maybe…' Andrea shrugged.

'It's okay. You can miss it more than a little.' They'd already talked about this. Cal had made sure that Andrea had really thought about her decision to move to London, and that it was what she really wanted. He trusted her, and knew that Andrea trusted him. That silenced whatever fears either of them might have.

She nodded. 'It's going to be difficult to leave. But it's time for me to move on; I want to come home.'

'We won't be doing that until you've finished up here. When I spoke to the board, they were more than happy to give me as much time as I need. I'll have plenty to keep me occupied here.'

'You're sure they're okay with that? This is an important opportunity for you, Cal.'

'I promised I'd be there for you, and I will.' Cal knew this wasn't easy for Andrea, and he wanted to make the transition as painless as possible for her.

'Thank you. I'm feeling better about it already.'

'Shall we take a stroll on the veranda? It's a beautiful evening.'

She nodded. 'Yes, that would be nice. Kissing you by the light of the moon.'

Cal went to fetch their coats, speaking to the waiter on the way back. When they sauntered out onto the deserted veranda, he could see the small table being prepared for them at the other end.

By the time they reached it the waiters had gone. Cal picked up the champagne bottle from the ice bucket, showing her the label.

'*Very* nice.' She nodded her approval.

'Joe suggested this vintage.'

'Ah. I see. So while Maggie and I have been getting excited about living in the same city, you and Joe have been discussing vintages, have you?'

They both jumped as the champagne cork popped, and Cal filled the two glasses that were standing ready. He'd meant to do this later on in the evening but he couldn't wait. Why wait, when they already had everything they needed?

'This was all my idea…' He fell to one knee, feeling in his pocket for the ring. Andrea almost dropped her champagne glass in astonishment, and he took it from her hand.

'We've made our commitment already. I'm never going back on that, and I want you to marry me, Andrea.'

'Yes. I want you to marry me too. I mean… I want to marry you back…' She was stammering now, her eyes full of tears. Cal caught her hand, bringing it to his lips, before he took the ring from his pocket.

'Cal…!'

'You're sure?'

'Yes! I'm sure.' She watched as he slid the ring onto her finger. 'It's so beautiful, Cal.'

'I knew this was yours the moment I saw it. You really like it?' Two diamonds, mounted together in a twined knot of gold. Inseparable, the way he and Andrea were.

'I love it. Thank you, Cal…' She pulled him to his feet, and Cal allowed himself the ultimate pleasure. He kissed the woman that he was going to marry.

EPILOGUE

A PAIR OF PEACOCKS strutted across the grass outside the large conservatory. Even the smallest details seemed to be conspiring to make Cal and Andrea's wedding day perfect.

The venue had needed almost no decoration because it was already stunning. The central paved area of the conservatory, which was now filled with chairs for the wedding ceremony, was surrounded by plants and greenery of all kinds. Orchids hung from the Victorian cast-iron framework that arched over their heads and Cal had even found a small area where medicinal plants were grown. He and Joe had joked that they might come in handy if anyone was taken ill.

On the other side of the grassed area was an old orangery, which was perfect for the reception. And on a day like today, the guests could join the peacocks outside in the warm sunshine.

Aunt Mae was sitting with Andrea's mother, dressed in fuchsia-pink with a large hat. Cal sat next to his best man, waiting for Andrea to arrive.

Joe patted the pocket of his waistcoat. 'I've got the rings.'

'Great. Thanks.'

'Everything's going to be fine, you know.' Joe reminded him of that fact for the umpteenth time.

'Yeah. Nothing to worry about.'

Joe sighed. 'Can't you just pretend to be a little nervous? I've read the book, and there's a whole chapter on ways that the best man can calm the groom's nerves.'

'Really? What does it say?' Cal couldn't think of one thing to be nervous about. Andrea would be here soon and they'd be married. That was all he needed to know.

Joe puffed out an exasperated breath. 'Tips and techniques, mate. If I told you what they were, they probably wouldn't work.'

Fair enough. Perhaps one of the tips was to appear nervous enough for both of them.

The last six months had had its share of ups and downs. Cal had watched Andrea's world begin to expand as she started to look beyond the boundaries of her mountain refuge, but still she'd shed a tear when they'd packed up all her belongings, ready to bring them home.

If he hadn't been so sure of her, his own confidence would have wavered. The first few weeks back in London had been difficult; she'd scoured the journals for a job and found nothing that suited her. Cal had wondered a few times whether he really could make her happy, but holding her at night never failed to quell his fears.

Then the right job had come along. It needed a special kind of person to work with children with disabilities and Andrea had agonised for days about whether she could do the job justice. But Cal had convinced her to give it a go and she'd come away from the interview fired with enthusiasm. The job offer had come two days later, and she hadn't looked back.

They were both changing and growing. Cal's new responsibilities meant he travelled much less than before, but when he did he knew that Andrea supported him in what he was trying to achieve. She'd taken time off work to accompany him on a trip back to Africa for a week, and sharing that had added yet another new facet to their happiness.

And he *was* happy. He'd never thought he had a right to anything this fulfilling, but now he could reach out and take it, knowing that Andrea was happy too.

'The cake's in one piece, at least.' Yet another of Joe's needless reassurances broke Cal's train of thought.

'The cake's the last thing we need to worry about. I *know* that's going to be great.' Maggie had insisted on making their wedding cake and Cal had heard that Joe had helped with the decorations. It had been a very special gesture and Andrea had been happy to let their friends decide on the design.

Joe shook his head. 'You might have warned me about this best man business. It's far more nerve-racking than actually getting married.'

'Don't worry. It'll all be over soon and you can relax.' Cal grinned at him. 'By the way, have you met Andrea's maid of honour? Her name's Maggie and I think you'd really like her.'

Joe finally smiled.

The music Andrea had chosen for her walk down the aisle began to play from speakers hidden amongst the foliage. Cal got to his feet, craning round to catch his first glimpse of Andrea, and saw Maggie coaxing the two little flower girls in the right direction.

Then he saw her, dressed in white lace with flowers in her hair. A lump rose in his throat as Andrea hurried down the aisle towards him, her father trying and failing to slow her down to a more modest pace.

And then they were standing together. He bent towards her, whispering in her ear. 'Let's get married, shall we?'

Andrea smiled up at him. 'Yes. Let's do just that.'

* * * * *

If you enjoyed this story, check out these other great reads from Annie Claydon

Healing the Vet's Heart
A Rival to Steal Her Heart
Winning the Surgeon's Heart
Best Friend to Royal Bride

All available now!